Danielle Hyland

LAUREN J. SHARKEY is a writer, teacher, and transracial adoptee. After her birth in South Korea, she was adopted by Irish Catholic parents and raised on Long Island. Sharkey's creative nonfiction has appeared in the Asian American Feminist Collective's digital storytelling project, *First Times*, as well as several anthologies including *I Am Strength!* and *Women under Scrutiny*. *Inconvenient Daughter* is her debut novel, and is loosely based on her experience as a Korean adoptee. You can follow her at ljsharks.com.

DISCARD

Westminster Public Library
3705 W 112th Ave
Westminster, CO 80031
www.westminsterlibrary.org

DISCARD

Westminster CO 80031

INCONVENIENT DAUGHTER

A NOVEL

INCONVENIENT DAUGHTER

DAUGHTER

A NOVEL

BY LAUREN J. SHARKEY

KAYLIE JONES BOOKS

This is a work of fiction. All names, characters, places, and incidents are a product of the author's imagination. Any resemblance to real events or persons, living or dead, is entirely coincidental.

Published by Akashic Books
©2020 Lauren J. Sharkey

ISBN: 978-1-61775-709-9
Library of Congress Control Number: 2019943818
First printing

Kaylie Jones Books
www.kayliejonesbooks.com

Akashic Books
Brooklyn, New York, USA
Twitter: @AkashicBooks
Facebook: AkashicBooks
E-mail: info@akashicbooks.com
Website: www.akashicbooks.com

Also Available from Kaylie Jones Books

Cornelius Sky by Timothy Brandoff
The Schrödinger Girl by Laurel Brett
Starve the Vulture by Jason Carney
City Mouse by Stacey Lender
Death of a Rainmaker by Laurie Loewenstein
Unmentionables by Laurie Loewenstein
Like This Afternoon Forever by Jaime Manrique
Little Beasts by Matthew McGevna
Some Go Hungry by J. Patrick Redmond
The Year of Needy Girls by Patricia A. Smith
The Love Book by Nina Solomon
The Devil's Song by Lauren Stahl
All Waiting Is Long by Barbara J. Taylor
Sing in the Morning, Cry at Night by Barbara J. Taylor
Flying Jenny by Theasa Tuohy

From Oddities/Kaylie Jones Books

Angel of the Underground by David Andreas
Foamers by Justin Kassab
Strays by Justin Kassab
We Are All Crew by Bill Landauer
The Underdog Parade by Michael Mihaley
The Kaleidoscope Sisters by Ronnie K. Stephens

For my mother, Katherine, who showed me what it means to be loved, and how to love, without limits.

For my father, Patrick, who taught me how to laugh with my whole body.

For my brother, Taylor, who helped me understand what it means to be family.

For my mentor, Kaylie, who believed in me.

And finally, for the love of my life, Bryan, who made me believe in second chances.

CHAPTER ONE

IF YOU'VE NEVER HATED YOURSELF and want to, do not correct them when they assume you've been raped. Accept kindness from the hardest nurse ever to work the ER as she hands you a clipboard and asks for identification. Hope no one will recognize you, for this wouldn't be the first time you were found somewhere other than where you said you'd be. Pray the answer is in your blood and it isn't too late.

"Rowan," the nurse reads, closing the curtain behind her, "you believe you were sexually assaulted?"

"No," I whimper as she wraps the nylon cuff around my right arm, "I was. I was fine and then he . . . I wanted to stop, but I couldn't—"

"Easy, easy," she says, finally looking up from the clipboard and placing a hand on my shoulder. "Take a deep breath for me, okay, Rowan?"

"Okay."

As the Velcro cracks against the silence, I try to calm myself.

"130 over 90."

"Is that bad?"

"It's a little high, but not too bad. Do you smoke?"

"No."

"Cigarettes, marijuana?"

"No."

"Do you drink?"

"No."

"But you drank last night?"

"Yeah, but I don't drink a lot, like, normally."

"And how old are you, Rowan?"

"Twenty-four."

"It says here you're on birth control."

"Yeah."

"Any other medication?"

"No."

"Any family history of cancer, diabetes, heart disease?"

"I'm adopted. No family history."

It was my first day at big-girl school, and we were late because my hair would not curl. Mom hit the brake of our tan Chevy Astro so hard I lurched forward in my car seat.

The night before, Mom had asked how I'd like to wear my hair for my first day. I remembered my fingers getting stuck in her dark brown curls, and asked for curls of my own. When she took the curlers out the next morning, I cried when I saw my hair was still straight.

"Don't cry, Rowan. You have beautiful hair. People would give anything to have thick, straight hair like yours."

She wiped my tears and separated my hair into two braids, promising if I kept them in all day and slept on them at night, my hair would be wavy the next day.

In the years to come, Mom would try different ways to give me the curls I wanted so desperately—Wash 'N Curl shampoo, ion curlers, and curling irons—but it always ended the same way: curly before I caught the bus, deflated by lunch, and straight by the time I walked up the driveway of our house on Elderberry. We didn't realize all I wanted was physical proof we belonged to one another—something tangible, an undeniable link.

I heard Mom breathing hard as she slid the door open, attempting to undo the seat belt. When I was finally undone, my Cinderella lunch box got caught in the straps, and I whined as Mom struggled to free me.

"Damn it," she said through clenched teeth.

"Mommy! You're not supposed to say that!"

"Shhh, Rowan! Come on, come on."

I saw boys and girls, in jumpers exactly like mine, going through two double doors and into a large building—their mommies alternating between waving goodbye and wiping their tears. Mom began to walk faster, dragging me behind.

"Mommy, slow down!"

Once inside, a wrinkled lady pointed down the hallway and said Mrs. Matthei's classroom was on the left. We sprinted down the hallway, and headed toward a room where we heard laughter.

"Hi," said a round woman with blond hair, freckles, and a smile, "you must be Rowan."

"Yes," Mom replied, "this is Rowan."

"It's very nice to meet you, Rowan. My name is Patty—I'm Mrs. Matthei's helper."

"Hi, Patty," I said, slightly cowering behind Mom.

"We're going to get started soon. Why don't you have a seat at the table with the green chairs—do you know which one that is?"

I nodded and pointed to the round table with lime-green chairs.

"Very good! Do you want to say goodbye to Mommy before she goes?"

Mom crouched down to meet me at eye level and hugged me tight.

"You're coming back, right?" I asked.

"Yes, I'll be back later, and I want to hear about all the fun things you do today."

"Mom?"

"What, sweetie?"

"I don't want to go here."

"Rowan, we talked about this," Mom sighed.

"I want to come home with you."

"Tell you what—you be a good girl for Mrs. Matthei and Patty, and there will be chocolate chip cookies when you get home, okay?"

"Okay," I said, squeezing her one more time. "Bye, Mommy!"

I ran past tables with blue, red, yellow, and purple chairs before sitting in the last available green chair, quietly taking in the room. The blackboard at the front of the classroom was blank, while the one on the far wall had a chart with each student's name, accompanied by small boxes to the right. I saw some boys and girls placing their backpacks into the cubbies beneath it but was too afraid to take off my backpack without permission.

I rested my head on the Cinderella lunch box Mom bought at the Disney Store especially for my first day, inhaling the scent of crayons and pencil shavings. The boys across from me were giggling and one asked, "Who is that lady?"

I followed his finger and noticed Mom was still at the front of the classroom talking to Patty and Mrs. Matthei.

"That's my mommy."

"Why don't you look like your mommy?"

"I don't know," I said honestly. "My mommy says I'm special."

"My brother is 'special.' He can't go to school with normal kids 'cause he's retarded. Are you a retard?"

"No!" I did not know what a retard was.

"She's adopted," the girl next to me explained. "My mom said your real mommy is in China but she didn't want you, so she gave you to a lady in America who can't make babies."

"Gross," the boy said, pushing his chair away from the table. "That's worse than cooties!"

The rest of the children pushed their chairs back—no one cared about my Cinderella lunch box with its matching thermos.

I looked at my mother. While I couldn't remember what color my eyes were, I knew they were not blue. They were not round. They were not hers.

I began to panic and attempted to fix myself by taking a deep breath and lifting up my eyelids as far as they'd go.

I simply didn't notice. Mom and Dad looked as they did, and Aidan and I looked as we did.

I'm not sure how Mom and Dad explained what it meant to be adopted. Even if I knew their exact words, at five you're too young to understand that fertility either strengthens or destroys a marriage, a dream . . . a person. You don't get that adoption isn't just a solution to a problem—it's arguments that last days and forms asking the same questions and home inspections. It's interviews and your call is very important to us. It's hormone injections and low sperm counts and old wives' tales and nonresponsive to treatment. It's what seems like yet another defeat in a long line of shit that isn't working.

It starts coming together when kids begin using their middle and index fingers to pull the corners of their eyes and laugh, "Me Chinese, me play joke—me put peepee in your Coke." It gets clearer when your classmates ask why you brought Irish soda bread in for Culture Day instead of fortune cookies. You are Asian to the people around you, but not to yourself.

I didn't know what it meant to be Asian, but it seemed everyone else did. They expected me to know karate, be good at math, and be able to use chopsticks, but I could do none of these things. As I moved through grade school, the novelty of my having slanted eyes and a permanent tan seemed to wear off.

I forgot the first time I met Mom was in an airport, and not in the delivery room of a hospital. I forgot the stick never turned blue for her, and instead, motherhood was delivered via phone call during my grandfather's wake—Rowan James, my father's father, after whom I was named. I forgot there was another woman out there I could call "mother."

Valentina and I gave each other knowing smiles as Sister Joan wheeled in the trolley. Despite the Panasonic being held in place by tension straps, Sister Joan still needed assistance to force the structure over the threshold that could not have measured more than half an inch in height. I found myself thankful Jessica Kautzman had transferred from Sacred Heart Academy, bumping me out of the first row, and sparing me the responsibility of helping Sister Joan work the VCR.

Unlike Mrs. Matthei's classroom, Sister Joan's was devoid of color and personality. Her desk, meticulously organized and questionably uncluttered, was at the far end, by the windows. It would later migrate to the center of the room, allowing Sister Joan a better vantage point to observe whether Valentina and I were passing notes.

Six rows of six desks each faced the blackboard, and the bookcase that shelved enough copies of the *New American Bible, St. Joseph Medium Size Edition*, for each Mercy girl.

Sister Joan looked as though she had been born cranky. I surmised she earned her wrinkles by perfecting the perpetual frown that sat between her nose and chin.

"Ladies, ladies!" she said, clapping her hands together. "No talking. While Miss Kautzman sets up the television, who can tell me who founded Our Lady of Mercy Academy? Yes, Miss Finelli?"

If there's one girl I hated at OLMA, it was Gianna Finelli. She got on at the last stop on the bus to Mercy, and always managed to hit me with her Jansport just as I had fallen asleep for the last half hour of the morning commute. I had this fantasy of yanking her black ponytail and hurling her onto the floor before using a Sharpie to connect her freckles.

"The Sisters of Mercy," Gianna answered, giving me the finger as my eyes followed Sister Joan down the middle row.

"That is correct! But who founded the Sisters of Mercy? Miss Aiken?"

"Catherine McAuley."

"Yes, *Sister* Catherine McAuley opened the first House of Mercy in Ireland in 1827. She wanted to use her inheritance to build a place where women could be sheltered and educated. Some of these women were un-wed mothers whose families had disowned them, which is why it's always important to practice abstinence."

Giggles.

"Ladies," Sister Joan said sternly, "there is nothing funny about abstinence and there is most certainly noth-ing funny about the consequences of premarital . . . relations."

Even at her age, the good sister couldn't bring herself to say the word.

"Many of the girls were no older than you are now—forced to live on the street, starving. Some of them with wee babes in their arms against the bitter cold. Yes, Randi, I see your hand—what is it?"

The class shared a collective groan. If there was one girl *all* of us hated, it was Randi. In fact, the amount of irritation she evoked incited us to begin calling her "Fuckin' Randi."

I guess our hatred had something to do with the fact that she didn't roll her skirt up like the rest of us, and her hair looked as though she'd only had enough time to run a brush through it once. Even though she was never tardy for class, she gave the appearance—and, un-fortunately, the odor—of someone running late. Perhaps it was because she wore a rosary—not Sarah-Michelle-Gellar-wore-a-rosary, but like *actually* wore a rosary.

"A girl from my church got pregnant and she's only fifteen and I think it's absolutely disgusting." Randi smiled triumphantly, as if never having kissed a boy was something to be proud of.

"Were you there when she got pregnant?" I muttered to Valentina.

Sister Joan's lips formed a tight line as laughter rippled through the rows.

I watched Randi smile and blink blankly, confused as to why my comment was so humorous. "What?" she laughed nervously.

It was then I realized we didn't hate Randi—we envied her. Despite her frizzy black hair forever being out of style, and the visible sweat stains of her white polo, Randi was completely secure in who she was. She didn't give a shit what we thought, and we wished we could be as confident as she.

"Do you have something to add, Miss Kelly?"

"Nope, nothing to add," I said, trying to suppress a smile.

"Getting back to you, Randi. Tell us more about this young woman at your church."

"Well," Randi began, clearing her throat, sitting up straight, basking in having the room's attention. She told us about how the girl tried to hide the pregnancy from her parents, how she still loved "the boy who did it to her," and how she was being sent away someplace upstate and would be back in a few months . . . without the baby.

Murmurs.

"Ladies, please—ladies, that's enough! Thank you for sharing with us, Randi. Understand this, girls—intercourse is meant to be an act of love. Genesis tells us, *A man shall leave his father and mother and be joined to his wife, and the two shall become one flesh*. Intercourse symbolizes two people becoming one in the hopes of having a child they may raise in God's image and likeness. This is why it is sinful to have relations before marriage. Not only is it sinful, but when young, unwed mothers find themselves with child—" Sister Joan inhaled deeply, clutching her rosary. "There is no greater sin than taking the life of another, except taking the life of a child. Abortion is never the answer, which brings us to today's presentation." She pushed the cassette into the VCR, which had *God Bless the Child* scribbled in blue pen across a piece of masking tape.

On the screen, I watched Theresa and her daughter Hilary move from shelter to shelter, sleeping on the streets when there were no beds, or when they didn't make it back to the shelter on time. After Hilary contracted lead poisoning, a social worker at the hospital told Theresa the only way Hilary could lead a normal life was if Theresa abandoned her.

Before they left the hospital, Theresa presented Hilary with a necklace.

"You know what that heart means?" she asked. "It means your mommy loves you. And whenever you look at it, that's what I want you to remember—your mommy loves you."

Theresa took Hilary to the park and placed her on the swings, promising to return with sandwiches. Then, hiding behind a tree, she watched social workers take Hilary, who called out for her mother.

I'd never given much thought to my biological mother since the first day of kindergarten. Yet here I was, nine years and one Cinderella lunch box later, shedding tears for a woman I'd never met.

Sister Joan tapped me on the shoulder and escorted me outside, leaving the door ajar so as to listen for mischief and unwittingly aid eavesdroppers. Her classroom was the last on the right, but there was still another on the left, plus three yards, before the end of the hall.

As we strolled past Sister Pat's geology lecture, I could feel the class's gaze follow us until we disappeared from view, though whispers and speculation still lingered.

I'd been in high school exactly two months, and already had a reputation. I rolled my skirt above the knee, chewed gum in class, and painted my nails black in the hope of getting expelled and being banished to Mineola High School and the boys who smoked Newports outside.

"What's the matter, Rowan?" Sister Joan asked.

Sister Joan knew she was my least favorite teacher, and that she was my least favorite teacher because she taught my least favorite class—theology. She'd written me more demerits than any other nun at Mercy—mostly for uniform violations. Two weeks prior to this conversation, she'd sent me home with a sealed envelope, which Mom was to sign and return. Enclosed was a copy of the dress code, with the following passage highlighted in orange: *Skirts are to be worn at the knee or slightly above the knee. Skirts are never to be rolled at the waist.* There was also a brochure on the relationship between modesty and abstinence. I'm not sure I confided in Sister Joan because I wanted to, or because fourteen years was too long to hold it in.

I told her I hoped this was how I came to be here— that my biological mother loved me and wanted the best for me, even if that meant we couldn't be together. That she knew it was better to give me to another family than have us suffer together. That she was willing to break her own heart so I'd never know the hardship she'd endured alone.

The bell rang and I watched the sea of navy and maroon sweaters funneling out of the classrooms and down the hall as Sister Joan took me in her arms and said, "Rowan, God sought fit to bless you with two mothers—your adoptive mother, and your biological mother, who loved you so much that she chose life, not death. She placed you in the hands of God, in the hope that He would provide a better life for you. You would not be here had she made a different choice, so you should rejoice that she was guided by faith, and that faith brought you here."

Sister Joan patted me on the back, and I followed her into the empty classroom to get my backpack while she wrote me a pass to see Guidance. By the time I got into the hallway, class change had ended, and I was alone.

The squeaking of my rubber soles echoed as I made my way to the stairs. Guidance was two flights up, but the answers weren't up there. The only person who could make this okay was in the house on Elderberry—Mom. I looked over my shoulder, and ran to press my cheek up to the door leading to the stairwell to make sure Sister Pat wasn't lurking in the halls, before heading to the basement.

All four locker rooms, the cafeteria, and the school store—which had three flavors of Charleston Chew but never any gum—were located in the basement. The upperclassmen's locker rooms always seemed to be maintained. I'm not sure if this was a budgetary thing, or simply because the freshman experience is congruent to a permanent state of figuring shit out, and the chaos that comes with it.

The freshmen lockers were bright red, layered two high, and smelled of feet and GAP Dream. Jessica Kautzman's transfer had landed me with a bottom locker, which was only a problem in the mornings when she popped her zits.

My backpack hit the ground with a thud. I pulled out my planner to see which books I'd need to take home when I noticed my neon-purple combination lock was on backward.

"Son of a bitch," I huffed, kicking the metal closet storing my books.

Gianna Finelli must have noticed I'd forgotten to lock up, and didn't want to waste the opportunity. I took a seat and kicked myself backward, my skin whining against the vinyl flooring.

Leaning my head against the locker, I rolled the dial three to the right, one long turn to the left, and a quick right. After packing my books, I walked to the other side of the room to locker 47. Of course, she'd fucking locked hers.

"Bitch."

I waited for the bell to ring, and made my way to the bus once Sister Monica began the afternoon announcements.

"Hey, Vinny."

"You're out early."

"Yeah, I cut last period."

"You keep doing that, you're going to wind up driving this bus," he said, taking a sip of coffee.

Vinny was a retiree who drank too much coffee and blamed his hair loss on the stress we girls gave him—not how he constantly ran his fingers through it once we got on the Long Island Expressway.

I rolled my eyes and realized I was first on the bus. Although I wasn't a senior, I walked to the back and tossed my backpack into the very last seat. I removed the navy-blue wool sweater identifying me as a frosh, and crammed it into my Jansport. Although just the polo made it ten degrees cooler, the combination of nylon tights and wool skirt wasn't making the unusually warm October afternoon any more bearable.

I hated this school, this uniform, this bullshit bus with its bullshit rules about freshmen needing to double up so seniors could have seats to themselves in the back. I hated theology class and God and that stupid movie. Most of all, I hated Mom for making me come here. For never letting me have a choice.

Mom was convinced I needed God and His rules. Every afternoon when I got home from school, she'd say, "How was your day, Rowan?"

"It sucked," I'd reply. "Do I have to go back tomorrow?"

"If you don't go tomorrow, then how are you going to get an education?"

"At Mineola High School," I'd reply.

Then she'd repeat the same line she'd given me the day we'd come to visit Mercy: "You wouldn't last one day in Mineola High School, Rowan."

"How hard can it be? You did it."

"Don't you have homework?"

The seniors piled into the bus and stopped midway through the aisle, pointing and whispering at my defiance.

"Take a seat, girls!" Vinny crabbed out. "We can't move until you take a seat."

For a moment, I got nervous that Lauren Ferro was going to make me move, but she just sneered and took the seat in front of me. I smiled and slid the headphones of my red Sony Walkman around my ears, turning the volume as high as it would go, and settled in. I hated the forty-five-minute bus ride too. As Mercy grew smaller in the bus window, I went back to my first visit to the school.

The summer before eighth grade, Mom enrolled me in a Catholic High School Entrance Examination (CHSEE) prep course at Chaminade, an all-boys Catholic high school less than a mile from our house.

Mom woke me at 7:20 on six separate Saturdays to shower, eat breakfast, and get in the car by 8:10, so I'd arrive by 8:17, and be at my desk by 8:30. Class would begin with a timed practice test, which we later exchanged with our neighbor to the left for grading.

These courses were marketed to middle-class parents and convinced them a Catholic high school education was sure to get their children to the Ivy League, the boardroom . . . to greatness. Like so many other Long Island parents, Mom was convinced a faith-based education was superior to the public school education of her youth, and the underachievement she felt it produced.

The relief I felt when the course finally ended was short-lived. Mom dragged me to Barnes & Noble where we purchased vocabulary flash cards, mathematics test books, and a wall calendar.

Beneath her Anne Geddes calendar of sleeping babes, Mom penciled in the names of every Catholic high school's formal open house—Our Lady of Mercy Academy, Kellenberg Memorial, Saint Anthony's—and they were all on a Saturday. Having worn a uniform the past eight years, I was hoping to ditch Catholic high school. But if I had to go—and it seemed I did—I wanted to go to Holy Trinity.

When my brother Aidan and I reached the age where our being home for the summer annoyed Mom, she decided to make us Mineola Summer Rec's problem. In exchange for what I assume to have been a substantial fee, the Village of Mineola provided its residents' children with the cheapest possible cotton shirts, whose insides would shed and stick to their skin. Distracted teenagers would gossip and blow whistles as we played kickball in a baseball diamond whose glory days were long behind it. On rainy days, we glued popsicle sticks together or made key chains out of lanyards.

Mom would come pick us up at two thirty p.m.—a faded, multicolored, polka dot and striped canvas bag crammed with towels slung over her shoulder, our pool passes hanging around her neck, and a jug of iced tea in her hand. Aidan and I settled in the front row of beach chairs on the second level, while Mom claimed the lounge chairs directly below us.

Aidan and I would squirm and jump impatiently as Mom slathered us with sunblock before we cannonballed into the deep end, washing most of it off. After we started to prune, we'd head back to Mom, who'd sometimes give us a few dollars to hit the snack bar and treat ourselves to french fries and Pepsi.

But most days, Aidan and I would drape our Power Rangers towels over two chairs, creating a fort that could shield us from the sun.

"What time is it?" we'd whine.

"Any minute now," Mom would say, flipping through her magazine.

We watched the entrance and waited for a mustached man with dark jeans, holes in his shirt, and a backpack full of tools to walk in after the little hand was between the four and the five, and the big hand landed on the six.

Even though we were always in the same spot, Dad would place his hand to his forehead to shield his eyes from the afternoon sun, and search for us. I'd see him first, and could never wait for Aidan before running to him.

The lifeguards would stand and blow their whistles, shouting, "No running!" as we sprinted into Dad's arms, not caring that he smelled of sawdust and sweat. We'd drag him to our spot, where Mom would be waiting with a kiss and his swim trunks.

Mom developed a permanent fear of water after seeing *Jaws*, but Dad could swim from one end of the pool to the other without coming up for air. His favorite thing to do was cup his hands under water, have us place our feet on top, and push off as he lifted up, sending us flying backward and making the biggest splashes.

By the time I hit sixth grade, the village had raised the Summer Rec tuition three times, and Mom began searching for alternatives. She finally enrolled Aidan and me in Holy Trinity's Summer Performing Arts Program. It was there I met my first Asian friend, Olan.

Olan was also adopted, but her parents had made a commitment to making sure she learned as much about her Korean heritage as possible. During one of our sleepovers, she tried to teach me how to use chopsticks and introduced me to kimchi.

Performing came easily, and I decided I wanted to become an actress. Trinity had a reputation for producing world-class performers. There was a rumor a junior was going to be on *Sabrina the Teenage Witch*.

Trinity had everything I needed to make it as an actress, plus boys and the only other person I'd met who looked like me, other than Aidan. On the CHSEE, you were allowed to list three schools, in order of priority, to receive your scores. Holy Trinity was at the top of my list.

Being that it was an all-girls school, Aidan, two years younger, got to stay home and watch cartoons the day of Our Lady of Mercy's formal open house. Mom hadn't stopped scolding Dad about his speed, forcing me to have my headphones on full volume. Suddenly, I noticed Mom's hand waving in front of my face.

"What?" I scoffed, attempting to swat her hand away.

"If I can hear your music, then it's too loud," she said, turning back to face the road. "Joe, I think you have to turn here."

"If it's not loud then I can't hear it over Dad's radio."

"Lower. It. Now."

"How much longer? It's been, like, an hour."

"We get there when we get there."

Our Tahoe turned into the parking lot of Our Lady of Mercy Academy twenty minutes later and found a place among MD and DDS license plates. We stretched and shook out the nearly hour-long car ride and joined the herd of North Shore families who had brought their daughters to the open house.

From what I could see, the school was four stories high, made of coral-colored brick, with a large tower in the center. The windows on the first floor were floor-to-ceiling, while the rest seemed to be a normal size. The building was surrounded by trees and sunlight—it was beautiful. But there were no boys at Mercy, and for me, this was a deal breaker.

"Why are there bars on the windows?" I asked as we made our way to the entrance.

"It used to be a boarding school," Dad began. "My mother was part of the original class of eleven in 1928, you know. By the Second World War, the sisters were doing their part with the rations and food stamps. I guess they put 'em up for protection."

"Isn't the war over?"

Rules were the backbone of Our Lady of Mercy: only seniors could take the staircase that ran down the center of the school, skirts were never to be rolled at the waist, all shoes must be purchased from the school's catalog.

"Faith is at the core of everything we do at Our Lady of Mercy Academy," Sister Margaret Ann, whose office I'd later come to frequent, began. "The education young women receive here is rooted in Christian values, and empowers them to use their God-given gifts to make a difference in the world."

It seemed like hours before we saw the Tahoe again.

"I don't want to go here," I said, slamming the car door shut.

"Watch that door, Rowan!" my mother shouted.

"I want to go to Trinity! I'd rather die than come here."

"Well, what if you don't get into Trinity? Then what are you going to do?"

"Why? Because I'm not smart enough?"

"Rowan, I didn't say that."

"Trinity is where I want to go. If I don't get in, then I'll just go to public school."

"You," Mom said turning to face me, "wouldn't last one day in Mineola High School with your attitude."

"Whatever. I don't want to go to Catholic school anyway—especially one where there aren't any boys. I'm an atheist!"

"Where'd you learn that word?"

"Nowhere."

"Don't you lie to me, Rowan Kelly. You tell me where you picked that up."

Silence.

"Fine, you don't want to talk? That's fine. Fine by me. Well, let me tell you what's going to happen: you're going to get out of this car, you're going to think about what you've said, and you're coming to Mass tomorrow and—"

"What? No, I'm not going to Mass!"

"You're going and then afterward we're going to ask Father Ken if he has time for confession because you need to get on the right path, Rowan Kelly."

When Vinny braked at my stop, I passed the seniors I'd displaced to the middle of the bus with a smirk, and hopped off the bus, determined. I came up the driveway slowly, wondering how I was going to start the conversation. After dinner, when the kids Mom cared for were done with their homework, but before the last kid was picked up, was ideal.

The house on Elderberry was one of two made of brick. One Christmas, an elderly woman wandered through our front door, handed Dad her coat, and Mom a cheesecake along with an index card with the recipe, in case it was her last Christmas. They both laughed as she realized she'd wandered into the wrong brick house, and the lady took back her coat and her cake, and came back for the recipe card an hour later.

After we lost Grandma Walker's cheesecake recipe, Dad decided it was time to give the house a more definitive look. He woke early one morning to head to the library, the lumber yard, and then Home Depot.

As I helped Mom set the table, we shouted to each other over the whine of the power saw and booms from the garage. Dad was covered in sawdust when he came in for dinner, and Aidan had gray paint all over his shirt.

Our directions to people who had never visited the house on Elderberry were always the same: *If you've hit the IHOP, you've gone too far. It's the one with the shark mailbox, you can't miss it.*

Walking up the gravel driveway, I thought about how weird it was that we never used the front door. We came in the back door, which opened to the laundry room. There was a black mat to the right, covered entirely by children's shoes. I took off my Oxfords outside to air them out before coming into the house.

The two sets of identical light-up Skechers belonged to the twins, Olivia and Julianna. I was surprised to see Jack's and Joey's matching Nikes—just different sizes— since they almost never stayed for dinner. My feet hurt just looking at Bethanne's penny loafers—I didn't miss Corpus Christi or its uniform.

As I headed into the kitchen, something caught my eye. A perfect pair of pink ballet slippers, which meant only one thing: Emma was here.

* * *

For a long time, I didn't think Mom had a job. Every morning as Aidan and I ate our cereal, Mom would stand behind me, comb out my knots, and try to make up for the fact that she could never give me curls. She learned to French braid, how to arrange butterfly clips, and I was the first girl in my school to wear a bra-strap headband. For my first middle school dance, she used a teasing-tail comb to make a zigzag out of my part and put my hair into high pigtails, just like Baby Spice.

When Aidan and I got home from school, there were always other children in our house—children whose parents had real jobs and couldn't pick them up from school. Since Mom didn't work, she took care of them. I thought this was pretty embarrassing.

We'd spread out across our kitchen table and Mom would put out chips or pretzels for us to munch on while we did our homework. Mom would give me a tiny Tupperware bowl, but the other kids got to eat out of the big Batman one. At dinner, I had to move down to the very end of the table, and I was the last to choose a treat even if my plate was cleared first.

I hated how Mom used to laugh when I claimed she loved the other kids more than she loved me. I hated that I had to go to school when all the other girls got to go to work with their moms on Take Your Daughter to Work Day. I hated how she'd hold up her finger for me to wait when she was talking and laughing and listening to the other kids describe their days at school.

"She doesn't love them more than she loves you, Rowan. That's crazy talk," Dad would say. "She works—"

"She doesn't work! She doesn't go to work!"

"She doesn't go to an office, but she works. She takes care of those kids so she can be here for you and Aidan."

"But she's not here. She doesn't pay attention to me when they're around."

"Rowan," he'd laugh, "your mother loves you so much. She loves you more than anything in this world. I wish you knew how special you are to her."

There was that word—special. By then, I knew "special" didn't mean special—it meant different.

In fourth grade, I volunteered to help Miss Lagalante bang the erasers at the end of the day. The chalk dust gathered in a cloud around me, attaching itself to my skin, making me paler. While Miss Lagalante ushered the children from our class down the hallway to the bus, I rubbed the erasers against my arms and face.

I sped to meet Mom in the parking lot with my arms wide. *Maybe we could buy chalk dust for me and Aidan—we could put it on in the morning and no one would think we belonged in China anymore.* I'd finally found a way to fix it.

"Rowan!" Mom screamed, putting her arm out to stop me from making contact. "What happened? What did you do? You're a mess!" She licked her hand and began brushing my cheeks and arms. "You're covered! Stand over there and get that stuff off you before you get in the car."

Mom had a talent for being angry with me one moment, then turning around with a happy face for the children she cared for. I watched her give the other kids smiles and hugs and high fives as they piled into our van, knowing I'd never be one of them.

* * *

The house was in full chaos when I got into the kitchen. The twins had just learned the repeat game, and Josie, our latest addition at just eleven months old, had opened all the cabinets in the kitchen.

"Rowan, can you go into the den and tell Emma I'm ready for her?"

"Ready for what?"

"She's going to help me roll the meatballs."

"Here," I said, going to grab an apron, "I can—"

"Rowan, she wants to help, I said she could help. Please, just let her know I'm ready."

"Okay," I sighed, defeated—not knowing my dislike of Emma would eventually develop into a fully formed and rationalized hatred. "But later can we—"

"Wait, before you do that, grab the milk from the fridge."

If anything had been new in our U-shaped kitchen, it was long ago. The vinyl flooring—a mock stone pattern of red, green, and orange blocks held together by a thin layer of gray—had begun to bubble from countless kids crawling, then walking, then running over it on their way past where Mom cooked, beyond the dinner table, and to the hallway, which led to the den and the toys we kept there.

Birch cabinets lined the left aisle—a foot of exposed brick between them and the ceiling—affixed with cast-iron handles, loose from years of yanking, on each side of the oven and the microwave above it. A window made up the middle run of the U-shaped layout, adorned with Heritage Lace Victorian Rose curtains Mom and Dad bought in Cape May.

The sink, however, was installed on the right aisle,

and not below the window, as is typically recommended. Dad installed two shelves above the sink for extra storage, and removed the backsplash so Mom could have a clear view of the table, and the children eating there, while she washed dishes.

"Where do you want the milk?"

"Just set it down there and get the cheese out."

"Can I ask you a question later?"

"What question? Is it about school?"

Rookie mistake. I thought prepping her for it now would make it easier, and now she wasn't going to let it go until she figured out exactly what I wanted.

"I don't want to ask now."

"Rowan, I'm extremely busy. I've got dinner on, I need to do the meatballs—what do you want?"

"It's nothing. Forget it."

"No, not 'forget it,' just—"

"I want to know about my real mother!" I blurted out.

Mom stood frozen—holding a wooden spoon in her left hand, and a pot holder in her right. Her blue eyes began to well, putting her flaked mascara in peril. At fourteen, I was officially eye to eye with her, but her dark-brown curls and low heels usually put her an inch or two above me. Even though she was making meatballs, she hadn't thought to put an apron over her white cable-knit sweater.

I watched my words work their way through her face—the wrinkles of her forehead fading from the sheer shock of it all. Mom always complained about having a hollow face—cursing her genes for not giving her fuller cheeks. As the tears escaped her eyes, they dropped off the edges of her cheekbones, instead of rolling downward.

The pasta water began to bubble over and sizzle against the stovetop as I searched for a way to take it back. I hadn't meant for it to come out that way. I knew she was my real mother—I don't know why I said it like that.

"I just," I whispered, sneaking past her trembling body to turn the flame down, "I just want to know if she—"

I couldn't find the words, so I went to get Emma.

The den was the last room Dad worked on before he called the house on Elderberry home. After it had been gutted, he let Aidan and me draw on the sheetrock before he installed the insulation and did the drywall. I used to wonder what the new owners would think when they found Aidan's and my scribbles lining the walls of their new home. Sometimes, I'd imagine taking a hammer to those walls, terrified I'd accidentally left a piece of myself there.

Emma, Julianna, and Olivia were lined up against the windows on the far wall. Each had her left hand on the window sill, and her right arm extended outward. Emma was first in line, wearing a black leotard and pink tights—her wavy brown hair twisted and pinned into a perfect bun.

"You stick your heel out, point your toes, and then slide your heel back in—like this," Emma demonstrated. "It's called a tendu."

Julianna and Olivia kicked their feet outward, lacking Emma's grace and precision. In my baby photo album, Mom has a picture of me in pigtails, wearing a Minnie Mouse leotard and white tights with red hearts. I'm picking at a wedgie and have a smile on my face—I am three years old.

Mom said Emma and I were twins because we were both born at the beginning of November, but I didn't see it. Emma was seven, and already perfect.

"Emma," I called out.

"Hi, Rowan!" the girls cooed.

"My mom's ready for you to help her with the meat-balls," I said flatly.

"Yay." Emma grinned, clapping her hands together and running past me into the kitchen.

Mom didn't say a word from the time she set the table to when she finished drying the dishes. Dad and Aidan must have thought we were having another fight since she wouldn't look at or speak to me when I asked if she could pass the Parmesan.

I ran upstairs to my room after doing my chores, and dropped my backpack before closing the door behind me. Turning to my desk, I shuffled college-ruled, loose-leaf paper, issues of *Cosmo Girl*, and CDs around—as if the way to undo it were underneath the clutter.

I pulled open the drawers of my dresser, shaking my bottles of CK One and Tommy Girl on their sides, and began shifting around my socks and underwear. When I didn't find anything, I riffled through my pajama drawer, my T-shirts, my keepsake drawer at the bottom.

Exhausted and slightly nauseated, I fell face-first onto my bed. I lay there for what seemed like a long time, before rolling onto my back. It was a little past six thirty p.m., and if I was going to watch *Dawson's Creek*, I needed to start my homework.

After sitting up, I caught sight of the crucifix Mom had hung above my half bath. I didn't believe in God, but I figured if He was truly out there, He'd help me. And so I closed my eyes and prepared to pray, when there was a knock at my door.

"Rowan," Mom called from behind the door. "Rowan, can I come in?"

"Yeah, Mom."

Mom entered slowly and quietly, walking across the pink carpet cautiously, as if she were afraid. Stopping at the foot of my bed, she looked to me for an invitation. I crossed my legs and folded them under, scooting to the head of the bed so she'd have room to sit.

"About what you asked me earlier . . ." She was speaking so low. "What is it you want to know?"

"Nothing," I lied.

"Rowan, it's okay for you to ask me things." She sniffled. "I just want you to know I love you very much," she said, holding her arms out.

"I love you too, Mom." I cried, falling into her.

"You're my daughter," she told me, stroking my hair and pulling me in close. "No matter what anyone else says, you're my daughter and I love you."

"I'm sorry," I wept.

She told me not to be sorry. She told me it was okay to be curious. She told me she was fine, but I knew I'd fucked up.

By acknowledging the existence of the woman who brought me into this world, I'd betrayed Mom. Asking about this woman I never knew somehow made her more real than the woman who kissed my boo-boos, packed my lunches, and did my makeup when I asked. As if

wanting to know about her meant I loved Mom less—
made Mom less.

I never asked about her again.

CHAPTER TWO

THE EXAMINATION TABLE FEELS COLD beneath me. I can't tell if it's actually cold or if the nurse is just shit at making people feel comfortable. It seems the entire staff's default setting is annoyed. Yet the melody of the ringtone that comes standard with every office multiline telephone, paired with the secretaries' robotic recitation of, "Winthrop Emergency, how can I help?" is strangely soothing.

"You're adopted?" the nurse repeats. It's the second time she's looked up from her clipboard.

"Yup."

"Where are you adopted from?"

"Korea . . . South Korea. You know, the only Korea that lets people out."

She laughs hard, and begins fanning herself with the clipboard. "Oh Lord, forgive me, but that was funny! You're too much, girl. Hop off that table and step onto the scale for me."

At twenty-four, I still can't step on a scale without trepidation and shame. As the nurse pushes the small weight farther and farther to the right, I wait for more questions. Nonadopted people always have more questions. They're fascinated and intrigued and curious and, as much as they'll never admit it, they're goddamn thankful. Thankful because people don't adopt unless they have to.

Aidan was scheduled to take the Catholic High School Entrance Examination one year after I asked Mom about my biological mother, or BioMom. I started calling her BioMom because I thought it would be funny to give her a name befitting a villain.

Three weeks before the exam, my parents planned to take Aidan to Saint Mary's open house after Mass, to see if he'd want to list it as one of the schools to receive his scores.

I convinced Mom not to make me go to Mass, under the guise of having to study for the PSATs, which seemed to be the sole topic of conversation for the entirety of my sophomore year. I was actually planning to call Valentina, who would then call Journey's—the shoe store where my cousin Chris and his friend Cole worked. This way, only Valentina's number would show up on the phone bill.

As I watched the car pull out of the driveway, I felt relieved I didn't have to spend an hour listening to the Gospel according to Luke and trying not to gag on stale Eucharist. Mom was starting to realize dragging me to church was more irritating than letting me stay home, and decided not to fight me on the atheism thing.

I tried to figure out when the last time we went to church as a family was, and realized it had to have been the previous Mother's Day. Even though it was Mom's special day, I kept asking why we needed to go to church. In a fit of aggravation, she had said, "Because we promised Aidan's biological parents we would raise him Catholic."

"What? Did you meet them?"

"No, we didn't meet them. They had specified it on his paperwork that they wanted him to go to a Catholic family."

"What about me?"

"Rowan, we're going to be late. Now *please* follow your brother and get in the car."

People liked to tell me it must have been a hard decision, that BioMom just wanted me to have a better life—that her sacrifice was the ultimate gesture of love. The box of important documents in my parents' bedroom could prove this for Aidan, but were there wishes for me in that box? I needed to know.

Despite being alone in the house, I checked over my shoulder before entering Mom and Dad's room. Stepping inside, I made sure to take note of every detail, knowing Mom would be able to tell if something were out of place. I found the key beneath her jewelry box, and unlocked the cabinet their TV rested on.

There were papers, envelopes, and folders crammed into every available space. I decided to grab from the top and place everything in a pile, one on top of the other, so I'd know how to reassemble them.

I flipped through tax returns, passport applications, old report cards, and then I saw a manila envelope—*R. Kelly* in Sharpie in Mom's handwriting. I fanned out its contents on the floor and began scanning the documents before finding a phone number. I dialed and waited.

The woman from New Beginnings Family and Children's Services told me her name was Liz, and asked how she could help me. I assumed she was used to the long pause that came after.

The silence continued longer than I expected, and she told me it was okay, to take my time—that she was here. I decided I was ready to speak, and rose to my feet.

"Tell me how I can help you," she repeated.

I explained I was adopted from her agency, that my brother's—"well, he's my brother but not like my biological brother"—biological parents gave instructions to my parents—"I mean, my adoptive parents"—about how they wanted him to be raised. "I just want to know if there's anything in my file . . . I just want to know . . . why?"

I provided what she asked for—date of birth, country of origin, last name. "So, from what I can see here, your birth mother surrendered you to Eastern. It's a very good orphanage—they provide excellent care. Truly, I can vouch for that—you got very good care."

This made no difference to me. It wasn't the answer I was looking for. "Yeah, but that doesn't explain why this happened to me."

"Honestly, a lot of these decisions are poverty-driven. Rich people don't give up their children for adoption. Most of these women are young, unwed mothers who want to avoid the social stigma of being a single parent and who simply cannot afford a child. Are you looking for a reunion? Because we can—"

"No. I don't want to meet her."

"Okay, that's fine—that's totally up to you. If you like, what some adoptees choose to do is write a letter to their birth mothers that we can place in your file. Just maybe telling her a little bit about yourself and that you're okay. This way, if she ever does reach out, it will be there for her."

"And what about me? Where's *my* letter? Is there one of those in my file?" I didn't wait for her to answer. "No, there isn't, because she's never come back for me. She didn't so much as leave a Post-it behind. She doesn't care what happened to me—she's not looking for me!"

Liz let me cry. I calmed down. It was almost over.

"Listen, before you go," she said, "I just want you to know that she knows your birthday."

"What?"

"Your birth mother—she knows your birthday. Every mother knows and, in some way, acknowledges that day, whether they give their child up for adoption or not. It's not something you forget. So, know that at least one day a year, she's thinking of you."

Without a kid, BioMom gets her life back. She can cut back on her shifts at the textile factory, go back to school, find a better job. On her lunch break, she can tap a stranger on the shoulder, let him know he's next in line. He can ask her out on two years' worth of dates before they move in together. Maybe they'll take one of those cheesy photos of themselves painting a wall for their *We've Moved* announcement card. She can say yes when he gets down on one knee, and not be plagued by sheer fucking panic when the stick turns blue a year from them. She gets a do-over. She gets a life.

And all I get is one fucking day.

CHAPTER THREE

"How old were you when you were adopted?"

"Three months."

"Oh, so you were just a baby." She smiles to herself—it's more of an observation than a question.

"Yeah."

"Have you ever tried to find your real mom?"

I want to tell her that my real mom is ten minutes away, having a cup of tea, and thinks I'm having lunch with Valentina. I want to tell her I don't need anything from BioMom—that I never needed anything. I want to tell her that twenty-four years is long enough for BioMom to get her shit together. I want to tell her that BioMom isn't trying to find me. I want to tell her BioMom could have other children. I want to tell her I know all this pointed to one simple truth—BioMom didn't want me and that's how I wound up in this exam room.

"No, I haven't."

At some point, every adoptee asks their adoptive parents this question. It's a trick question—the adopted equivalent of, "Do these jeans make me look fat?"—and all adopted kids know the answer. I decided to ask during Sunday dinner. I was fifteen, and the need for an answer had been building within me since my conversation with Liz from New Beginnings.

Before leaving for seven o'clock Mass each Sunday morning, Mom would set the dinner meat on the counter to defrost—chicken, roast beef (Dad's favorite), turkey. That particular Sunday was chicken.

Mom started peeling the potatoes around three p.m. Once the potatoes were boiling, she skinned and chopped the carrots before transferring them into a round, clear Pyrex casserole dish. After adding a few tablespoons of water, she steamed the carrots in the microwave before preheating the oven. Dinner wouldn't be for another hour and a half, but Mom knew she couldn't use the oven and the microwave at the same time without blowing a fuse. Once the aroma of garlic and thyme wafted up the staircase, Aidan and I knew it was time to set the table. We'd race down the stairs, using the wall to steady ourselves as we rounded the corner, bypassing the hallway leading to the den, and into the kitchen.

A wooden bench sat on each side of the kitchen table, with Mom's chair at the head. Dad and Aidan sat against the wall, with me on the opposite side. Dad always groaned when Aidan inevitably asked if Dad could slide out so he could go to the bathroom just as Dad finished arranging his plate.

The Jets must have been playing that Sunday. We were relatively quiet around the table—save for Dad's random "pass it" and "come on." I decided to wait until Dad went for his second helping of mashed potatoes before making my move.

"Mom," I began.

"Yes, Rowan?"

"Never mind."

"What?"

"Nothing, forget it."

"What is it, Rowan?" she asked, setting her fork and knife down.

"Would you have adopted me if you and Dad could have had your own baby?"

Dad was still holding the ladle, looking at Mom, and Mom looked at him. Aidan's eyes were on me, and I could feel Mom's begin to do the same.

"Of course we would have adopted you, Rowan," Dad laughed.

"Then why did you try to get Mom pregnant if you knew you were going to adopt?"

"Because . . ." he stalled, hoping the gravy pouring down the mountain of mashed potatoes would somehow spell the answer.

"If you and Mom could have had a baby, would you have adopted me and Aidan too?"

"Rowan!" Mom screeched, slamming her hand on the table. "We love you and your brother very much. Your father and I could not have children, so we decided to adopt. Now, hand me your plate."

In addition to setting the table, it was also Aidan's and my job to clear the table. The first time we did this, Dad laughed at our inefficiency. We took our plates in our hands, walked into the kitchen, and placed them on the counter next to the sink for cleaning, one at a time. The next day, Dad instructed us to use a fork to scoop any scraps onto one plate, then place the cleared plate beneath it. Once we were done, we could stack the silverware on the top plate, and bring the stack in one trip.

Then we'd hand the silverware to Mom, and scoop all the scraps into the garbage so as not to clog the sink.

Not tonight.

Mom snatched my plate and smooshed it on top of Dad's, mashed potatoes coming off the sides. Her plate crashed on top of mine, and Aidan quickly surrendered his. She carried them into the kitchen, and began running water over them.

"Don't you have PSAT review sheets?" she asked.

I rolled my eyes and marched upstairs to my room, slamming the door behind me.

"Watch that door, Rowan!" I heard her shout.

I sat on the floor and leaned back against my bed. On the nightstand to my right was a picture of the four of us at Lake George. Aidan is about three, which means I must've been five, going on six. Dad has his arms around me; Mom is smiling, balancing Aidan on her hip—our tan skin dark from hours in the lake under the sun, theirs red from sunburn.

We were the solution to a problem—a last chance, a safety school, the store-brand version of procreation. The women whose wombs bore us didn't want us . . . and neither, really, did the woman we called Mom.

Maybe it was hormones. Maybe it was going to an all-girls Catholic high school. Either way, as I approached the end of my sophomore year at Mercy, I found myself desperate for a boyfriend. I'd also fallen hard for Valentina's brother Nicolas.

Valentina and her family moved to the United States from Uruguay when she was ten. Nicolas was two years older, and should have been a senior at Mineola High

School, but was repeating his junior year just as Valentina and I were about to be juniors.

The summer before Valentina and I officially became upperclassmen, Nicolas kissed me.

I'd gotten up in the middle of the night during one of our sleepovers to get a glass of water. He was sitting at the kitchen table with no shirt on and asked if I wanted to "chill" with him. I went to sit across from him when he grabbed my arm and pulled me close, patting his thigh.

I slid onto his lap, and began to blush, suddenly embarrassed to be wearing a SpongeBob T-shirt and matching shorts.

"What's wrong? Are you scared?"

"No," I lied. "Why would I be scared?"

"I don't know," he chuckled. "Sometimes people get scared at night."

"Not me."

"So tell me, *Rowan*—what are you doing up so late?"

"Nothing—just getting a glass of water."

Without warning, he pressed his lips against mine. His tongue pushed through my lips as his hands squeezed my waist.

"Wait," I sighed.

"What's wrong?" he panted.

He looked beautiful—his black hair was disheveled to reveal tiny patches of gray, like his father's. His eyes were warm, brown—kind. They seemed worried they'd gone too far, that I didn't feel the same, that I didn't want this too . . . but I did.

"I should get back to bed."

When I woke the next morning, there was a note under my pillow: *X-Men Friday?* with boxes next to the words *yes*, *no*, and *maybe*. I checked *yes* and slipped it under his door while Valentina showered.

On Sundays, Mom stayed in her room, catching up on her shows, while Dad screamed at the Jets a floor below. After Valentina's mom drove me home, I knocked on Mom's door to tell her I was back. She must have known something was amiss when I didn't immediately retreat to my room after telling her about my weekend.

"What do you want, Rowan?" she asked, pausing the TV.

"Mom, can I go on a date?"

She considered the question carefully. "Why? Has someone asked you on a date?"

I suppressed the urge to roll my eyes. Seriously, like I was going to fall for that.

"No," I lied. "But if someone does, can I say yes?"

"Honestly, Rowan—you're too young to date. You can start dating when you're sixteen."

I felt faint for a moment.

The cutoff for school registration on Long Island was usually in late November. This always left one or two December babies in each grade who should have been in the grade above. My birthday is November 5, which left me on the opposite end, usually the last to turn a year older.

Sixteen was almost four months away.

"Sixteen? But that's forever from now!"

"Then that gives you plenty of time to find a nice boy to go out with."

"Well, Valentina's brother sort of likes me—"

"No," Mom said flatly. "He's too old for you."

* * *

Mom was furious when Mrs. Kirk caught me making out with Nicolas at the Broadway Mall Multiplex, and grounded me for a month—no phone, no TV, and no more sleeping over at Valentina's house. Two weeks into my punishment, Nicolas started dating a sophomore from Mineola High School.

That's when I stopped telling Mom things.

The summer between sophomore and junior year was the first Mom hadn't scheduled. Her only rule was an hour of the assigned summer reading every morning when I woke up, and every night before going to sleep. Aidan's eighth grade teacher had labeled him a "bad test taker" and, as a result, he was enrolled in a more intensive Catholic High School Entrance Examination prep course at Chaminade. My days were my own—I had absolute freedom.

Valentina and I both lived in Mineola and wanted out once I became officially ungrounded at the end of July. Mineola's Main Street was eight blocks south of Jericho Turnpike, where all the presidential streets began. It consisted of one deli that never seemed to be open, the Saint James Restaurant whose food sucked no matter how many times it switched owners, and a bakery with no tables. The rest of Mineola was an endless strip of nail salons, pharmacies, and banks separated by 7-Elevens, Dunkin' Donuts, and other places to get subpar coffee.

On weekends, Valentina and I took turns hanging out with the various girls we ate lunch with at school. If we had money, we'd take the Long Island Rail Road to Oyster Bay to see Sophia, or to Huntington to hang out with Madison.

Previously, I'd been under the misapprehension that anything north of Old Country Road was the North

Shore, and everything south was the South Shore. It wasn't until I went to Mercy that I learned the North Shore, popularly known as the Gold Coast, was the collection of old-money towns bordering the Long Island Sound. The families who lived there belonged to yacht clubs, drove Bentleys, and threw their daughters cotillions *and* sweet sixteens. However, most Saturdays we were broke and ended up at the mall.

Laura, the latest addition to our corner table in the cafeteria, was from Hicksville and, like us, wasn't beholden to the distinction of living on the North or South Shore. Our towns were somewhere between the two shores, and didn't reveal enough about ourselves to warrant any real judgment.

Laura lived a mile south of the Broadway Mall, whose only real draw was the movie theater and the IKEA, which seemed to be preventing its demolition. Half the stores weren't even open, the security guards began kicking people out a half hour before closing, and the food court only had a Subway, an Arby's, and a McDonald's. Laura believed her mall was the superior mall. But as all Long Island natives know, there's only one mall worth going to, and that's the Roosevelt Field Mall.

Every Long Island native will tell you the Roosevelt Field Mall ranks differently on the list of largest malls in the country. Most say it's number three, but last I checked, it was somewhere near tenth place. Either way, at a little more than two and a half miles from Valentina and me, and only a $1.75 bus ride for Laura, the Field was our preferred hangout. Not only could we choose from Auntie Anne's Pretzels, Häagen-Dazs, and Jamba Juice, but I could see Cole.

Cole was my cousin Chris's best friend. Chris usually worked the closing shift at Journey's on Saturdays, and never said no when Valentina and I asked for a ride home, after making sure Laura got on the bus all right. Valentina would try on every type of sneaker they had while I flirted with Cole over the counter.

One Saturday, on the way home, Valentina and I begged Chris and Cole to take us to a bar where they were meeting some people after they dropped us home.

"Rowan," Chris scoffed, "you can't even drive. What are you going to do at a bar?"

"Um, get drunk, obviously," I pouted.

"Have you even had a drink before?"

"No," I said. "The only ID I have is my school one."

This seemed hilarious to Cole and Chris, and it took them a few minutes to stop laughing.

"Tell you what," Chris said, still laughing. "Cole here will hook you guys up with the same guy who did our IDs, and if you can keep a 40 down, you can come to the bar with us."

"You're on!"

Cole and I finally kissed the weekend after the SATs. It happened in the stock room of the Journey's where he and Chris earned their weed money. Even though I was sixteen, at nineteen with green hair and a Donnie Darko hoodie, Cole wasn't who Mom had in mind when it came to dating. He towered above me at six feet and one inch, and had eyes a deep shade of evergreen. They constantly had dark circles beneath them, like he never got enough sleep. The wallet at the end of the chain hanging from his jeans held our fake IDs.

"You just missed your cousin," he said as I entered the store, high-fiving me.

"Where is he? It's almost nine."

"Can't get here soon enough," he said, lowering the gate.

"He's coming back, right? I told my mom I'd get a ride with him."

"Relax," he laughed, "he just went to smoke a bowl real quick."

"Cool." I put my hands in my pockets and walked the perimeter.

"So," he whispered, "you want to see them?"

"Yeah!" I said excitedly. I met him by the register where he slid two IDs across the counter.

"They look nothing like us!" I screamed.

"Shhh, not so loud," he hissed.

"Oh shit, sorry," I said, lowering my voice, looking toward the stock room. "Is someone back there?"

"No, but I don't need one of the rent-a-cops walking by and catching a peek at them."

"Are you sure these are going to work?"

"Mine does," he shrugged. "Why do you even need one anyway?"

"I don't know. Valentina and I just want to try it, that's all."

"You're never going to get into a bar with one of those," he laughed.

"We're not going to a bar." It was my turn to laugh. "We just want to go to the liquor store and get some Zima or something. We've never been drunk before."

"Ha! Well, you're definitely not going to get drunk on Zima."

"Then what would you suggest?"

"I'll tell you when you're older," he chuckled.

I put the IDs in my pocket and strolled around to the other side of the register. "Hey, can I see the back?"

"Sure, why not?"

I followed him through the stock room and down the aisle of various Sketchers, Converse, and Nike boxes that reached to the ceiling.

"That's a whole lot of sneakers."

"Yeah."

"How's Chris going to get in if the gate's closed?"

"He'll call."

At the very back of the stock room was a refrigerator next to an emergency exit, and a small table covered in condiment packets shoved in a corner. I brushed them to the side to make room and sat on top, my feet swinging.

"What should we do until he gets back?"

Cole looked at my chest and I took a deep breath like I'd seen girls in the movies do to make themselves look sexier—he noticed and moved closer.

"Do you . . . want to make out?"

"Okay."

I didn't understand why I was nervous. Nicolas and I had made out three times, and I even let him feel under my bra, but this was different.

I wasn't worried about what would happen if Chris found out. It didn't occur to me this would have consequences on what could have been a lifelong friendship. I was fifteen, and wasn't concerned about what the kiss would mean past this moment. I was simply afraid he would change his mind and walk away.

He placed his hands on my shoulders and began trac-

ing the length of my arms with his fingertips before pulling my hands upward so we were palm to palm. Fingers
intertwined, he leaned forward, and I closed my eyes.

Cole kissed me with care and precision—as though
he had the instructions Nicolas didn't. Suddenly, I understood desire.

I broke the hold and clenched my fists around his
hoodie, desperately attempting to get a grip on anything
that would bring him closer. His hands seamlessly relocated to my jeans' back pockets, pulling me in. We
gasped for air between kisses, afraid to stop even for
a moment—as if we'd been waiting our entire lives for
this kiss, and weren't sure we'd be here again. And then
it was over.

Cole ran to let Chris in. They dropped me at the house
on Elderberry and went off to do whatever it is nineteen-
year-old boys do on Friday nights after the mall closes.

Before we lived in the house on Elderberry, we called the
Tudor on Weybridge home. Mom used to load me into
the stroller and push me down the three-quarters of a
mile to the mall. Once there, we'd go up and down the
storefronts before stopping at the food court where we'd
share a Coke, a pretzel, and a hot dog.

Now the only reason I went to the mall with her was
because she always bought me something.

Mom and I were walking past Delia's at the start of
junior year when I saw the gown—strapless, red, with
a sprinkling of gems along the sweetheart neckline, and
just enough poof to make a girl feel like a princess and
still be able to get through the doorway.

"Mom," I called out.

She took a few steps backward. "Very nice. Where are you going to wear it?"

"Nowhere, I guess." I had been sixteen for a month, but had no one to ask to the Sadie Hawkins Dance at the end of March, and senior prom was a year away.

"Why don't you try it on?"

"What? No, let's go!"

"Just come in and try it on," she said, halfway into the store, me trailing behind her.

Mom was already at the counter by the time I bobbed and weaved my way through groups of giggling girls looking to spend their allowance, and college students who hadn't quite outgrown clothing that shed glitter.

When it came to shopping, Mom's drink of choice was shoes. She could spend hours in Nine West, Steve Madden, and Aldo. But with clothes she was different. If we were on a mission for something specific—Bermuda shorts for a cruise, a light denim shirt dress for summer—we were in and out. Yet, no matter how many bags we had or how long we'd been at the mall, she never rushed me or said no to any of the stores I wanted to go to. More than that, she always managed to scrounge together a few dollars so I had something to carry up to my room and hide from Dad when we got home.

The cashier—whose name tag read *Chelsea* and was covered in Lisa Frank stickers—had five different bottles of nail polish open, and was fanning her right hand, while trying to balance the cordless between her cheek and left shoulder. Mom constantly gave people the benefit of the doubt and waited to be acknowledged.

Chelsea continued to ignore us, and laughed loudly at whatever the person on the other end was saying.

"Excuse me," Mom finally said.

"Um," Chelsea said, moving the speaker away from her mouth, "yeah?"

"We'd like to try on the dress in the window."

"It's over there," she pointed, and returned to her conversation. "Yeah, I'm at work. I don't know."

"Excuse me," Mom said firmly. It was a tone I knew well, and I felt sorry for Chelsea. She was in trouble and didn't even know it.

"Yeah?"

"We're going to need help finding a size."

"I'm going to have to call you back," Chelsea huffed. The phone beeped as she pressed the red button and set it down on the counter. "All the sizes are on the tags. Anything else?"

Mom's right leg stiffened as her left leg snapped outward and she crossed her arms—her fighting stance. "Is there a manager who can help us?"

The word "manager" reminded Chelsea she wasn't in her bedroom talking to her own mother, but was actually at work, in a store, and was required to help people. Chelsea nearly leaped over the counter and apologized again and again as Mom smiled and assured her it was okay. It was definitely not okay.

For the finishing touch, Chelsea unlocked the large fitting room at the end of the hall and hung the dress on the back of the door. "Just give a shout if you need anything."

Mom thanked her and turned to me. "Do you want me to come in with you?"

"No, I got it," I said, and closed the door.

"Come out and let me see you," Mom said, knocking on the fitting room door when I didn't immediately emerge.

"Give me a minute!"

"Excuse me?" *There's that tone again.*

"I mean, just wait a second. I can't get the thing into the other thing."

The doorknob began to jiggle and I immediately threw my body against it. "Mom!"

"What?" she laughed. "You think I don't know every inch of you by now?"

"Fine," I said, retreating.

She stepped into the room and motioned for me to turn so she could fasten the clasp at the top of the zipper. Then she had me stand in front of the mirror. "Rowan," she sighed.

I knew she wanted to touch me, but she held back. She just stood there and smiled—I wondered if we were seeing the same thing.

I wasn't disappointed or upset when we left empty-handed. I didn't have anywhere to wear it.

My favorite thing to do after coming home from Mercy was taking off my Oxfords. Once I kicked them onto the back deck, I removed my knee-highs, tossed them over the bannister, and sprayed them with Lysol. I'd drop my backpack onto the mat and rub my sweaty feet on the memory foam rug meant to catch dirt.

My feet would squeak as I sped up the hardwood stairs, and I'd roll my eyes when Mom called out, "Watch those doors, Rowan Joy!"

That day, I did kick my shoes onto the deck. I did toss the knee-highs over the railing. I did spray them and I did squeak up the stairs, but I didn't slam the door. Instead, I was frozen in the doorway.

The bag was under my desk—perfectly white, with *Delia's* written across in silver foil. I got down on my hands and knees, grabbed the bag, and placed it on my desk. I slowly untied the knot, and opened the bag.

"You'll find somewhere to wear it to, and someone to wear it for," Mom said behind me.

I came to my feet and gave her a hug—a real hug—hoping the intensity of our embrace would temporarily fuse us together so she could feel my love and know it was real. Despite having no occasion and no date, she knew it wouldn't always be that way. She believed I was a worthy investment—that someone else would see my value. With this dress, she said, someone—someday—would want me.

CHAPTER FOUR

I CAN'T HEAR NURSE MURMURING my weight over the sound of Dr. Mueller being paged over the loudspeaker. Before I can ask, Nurse has already moved to the next line and raised the height rod.

I can't tell if she is simply on autopilot or just wants to go home. Her Snoopy scrubs are faded from years of taking vitals. She presses her right hand against her eye while her left lowers the height rod. I wonder if she sees me.

"Sixty-four inches—you can step off the scale now. You have any brothers or sisters?"

"A brother—Aidan."

"Is he your—"

"He's adopted too, but no, we're not biological brother and sister."

"Wow," she smiles to herself, "that's amazing. You two are truly blessed and that's all there is to it."

Aidan's caller ID photo is one I took of him on one of our family's trips to Colonial Williamsburg. Those who know him often joke Aidan suffers from "carcolepsy," since his eyes close as soon as whatever vehicle he's in goes into drive. I don't know why I decided to snap a picture of him that day, but the image of him in a blue-striped hoodie, hunched over, wearing a white baseball cap, remains permanently attached to his name in my phone.

I rarely see it. When Aidan calls it's for two reasons: 1) he needs a ride to or from somewhere, or 2) he can't get in touch with either one of our parents. There's no other reason for him to contact me.

I remember when Mom, Dad, and I went to get Aidan from the airport. It was snowing and I was busy playing with my pink plastic tea set. Someone told me it was time, and I rushed down the stairs of the Weybridge Tudor and into the car. I was anxious to get moving since the next time we walked through the door, there was going to be a baby and he would be my brother.

At two years old, I thought this was how families were made. There was a mommy and a daddy, and the airport was where children were kept. I didn't know two people had to decide they wanted children—that they had to consider if they were ready for this. I didn't know those same two people would attempt to create life with their own bodies and fail. I didn't know this baby wasn't my "real" brother.

The only thing I knew about siblinghood was I was required to love this human because we shared the same last name. I found this difficult since Aidan never seemed to stop crying. He cried for what seemed like entire days, to the point where Mom would place him in the crib, lock herself in the bathroom, and pound the back of the door with her fists to keep from going insane.

First, he had scabies, then an ear infection. Aidan also

had two holes near a place called "the soft spot" that seemed to make Mom upset.

One day the crying stopped. One day he could walk and talk and play, and it appeared as though all Aidan wanted to do was make me happy. He watched the movies I wanted to watch and played the games I wanted to play. Whenever Mom and I would argue, I'd plan to run away. He'd start to cry and ask if he could come with me.

"No," I'd say, packing my Powerpuff Girls backpack, "but I promise I'll come back for you."

Then high school came, and with it, the divide.

I thought he was angry about me going to Our Lady of Mercy Academy, leaving him as the only Asian in Corpus Christi Elementary. Perhaps it was because my homework was so extensive, I didn't have time to help him beat Donkey Kong. Either way, I found myself angry as well.

Mom and I had declared war on one another. The kitchen and the second-floor hallway between my room and my parents' room became our battleground. Our fights were born over the dinner table, stomped up the stairs, and ended with the slamming of both our doors.

I felt betrayed when Aidan would ask why I couldn't just be nice, why I had to lie . . . why I couldn't follow the rules. He backed Mom up even when she was wrong.

I thought Mom loved Aidan in a way I never thought she loved me. He always managed to say, do, and eat the right thing. Their relationship was easy, effortless—natural. He didn't lie about where he went, who he was with, what he was doing—he didn't have to. Aidan was perfect to Mom—and I hated him for it. So, I started asking for a sister.

The sound of laces tapping against steel-toe Timberlands gave Dad away before he knocked on my door. With the SATs behind me, I was free to spend weeknights journaling my plans to get Cole to fall in love with me.

"Come in," I said.

"You know," he began, closing the door behind him, "I built you this beautiful desk, so I don't know why you sit on the floor to write in your diary."

"It's not a diary, Dad—it's a journal!"

"Is that so?" As he lowered himself to the floor, he let out an exasperated sigh—bending and kneeling after a day's work on the job site was not as easy as it used to be.

"Diaries are for stupid girls—journals are for writers."

"Potato, potahto," he laughed. "Anyway, I heard you're going to a dance?"

"And?" I said impatiently. "And?!"

"And your Mom says you can go out with your friends after, but you have to be home by eleven p.m., you understand?"

"Oh Dad!" I screamed, falling into him.

"That means 11:00 p.m. exactly, Rowan. Not 11:01 or 11:02, you got it?"

I let go of him and rolled onto my back. "I can't believe it. How'd you get her to say yes?"

Dad was a carpenter—he built a home for us to live in, decks for our neighbors, a desk for me to write on. After dinner, he could be found falling asleep in front of the TV to the sound of Jack Bauer interrogating bad guys. I'd wake him, and ask about a slight bend in the rules Mom had set for my existence. Dad would say he wasn't going to make any promises, only to show up in my room with good news a few days later.

"Rowan, Mom loves you. She wants you to go out and have a good time."

"No, she doesn't. She just wants me to stay here, in this room . . ."

"Hey, hey, hey. I'm telling you true. She loves you, Rowan, so it wouldn't kill you to say thank you. Now here," he said, holding his hand out, "help your old man up."

I took his hands in mine, and pulled back. Once he was up, he placed his hands on his hips and inhaled deeply, extending his stomach forward.

"Daddy?"

"Whatty?"

"I don't know if I want to go anymore."

"What?" he laughed, raising his hands to his head. "You are just like your mother, I swear, Rowan."

"Well," I said, crossing my arms against my chest, "I'm scared."

"Of what?"

"I CAN'T DANCE!"

"What are you talking about? You go to those Chaminade dances all the time. You're telling me you listen to all that Backstreet Kids and Britney Aguilera crap for the *lyrics*?"

"Yeah, but I can't, like, fancy dance. No one ever slow dances with me. I can't dance and I'm not going!"

"Come on," he said, flinging the door open.

"Where?" I asked, as I followed him through the hall, down the stairs, and into the living room.

He stopped by the stereo, and began scanning the CD tower.

"Mom's going to kill you if you get sawdust all over the living room."

"You let me worry about that. Now, come here," he said, inserting a CD and pushing play.

"Now *that's* music." He closed his eyes, humming along.

"Dad, this sounds old."

"Shut up and stand right there," he said, pointing no more than two feet in front of him. "A lot of people think you have to get fancy with the dancing, but really, all you have to do is the opposite of what I do."

"What?"

He took my hand and pulled me closer, setting his hand on my hip and my left hand on his shoulder. Then, our opposite hands joined together.

"So, when I move side to side, you just do what I do. But if I step backward?"

"I step forward."

"That's it—you got it."

"Are you sure there isn't more to it?"

"Ah, be quiet—this is the best part."

He broke his hold to turn the stereo up, then came back to pick up where he left off.

"*The summer wind*," he sang, "*came blowin' in, from across the sea. It lingered there, to touch your hair, and walk with me.*"

"Dad, they're not going to play this old crap at the dance."

"Doesn't matter," he smiled, spinning me out and back, "it's all the same language."

"Well, obviously," I said, rolling my eyes.

"Rowan, it doesn't matter if it's Sinatra or the Spice Dream—they're all singing about the same thing."

After "The Way You Look Tonight" and "I Won't Dance," we walked into the kitchen. Dad grabbed two glasses and poured us both some milk while I hopped on the counter and put peanut butter on two spoons.

"Sometimes there's nothing better than peanut butter and a cold glass of milk."

"Daddy?"

"Whatty?"

"What do I do at the diner?"

"Well," he laughed, "I heard a rumor they give you a book with all the things they make and you pick—"

"Dad!" I said, hitting his arm. "I mean, what do I do when the check comes? Do I pay or does he pay? I asked him to the dance so does that mean I pay?"

"You never pay for a date, Rowan!"

"But I don't know if it's a date. It's not like I can ask him if it's a date, Dad."

"How are you getting to the dance? Is Valentina's brother giving you guys a ride?"

"I told Mom already—Cole drives so he's picking me up."

"If he's coming here, to this house, and taking you, my daughter, to the dance and bringing you home, then it's a date."

"Okay, but still."

"If he's a gentleman, he's going to pay. If he's a bum, he'll split the bill and you'll never see him again."

I suddenly became very worried about what type of guy Cole was. "How am I going to know if he's going to pay the whole thing?"

"Relax, don't get so excited. I'll teach you another dance—the check tango. Or, the *chango*," he giggled to himself, tossing his spoon into the sink.

"What is that?"

"You offer to pay three times and then after that, if he still insists—which he should—then it's his check. And that's across the board—you go out with your girlfriends, and one of them offers to pay, they refuse you three times, and that's their check, you understand?"

"Do I ask him three times *before* we order or when the check comes?"

"Here's what you do: when the check comes to the table, pick it up. He'll take it from you—that's one. After he opens it, you go into your purse and get your money out. He's going to tell you to put it away—that's two. Then you laugh a little and say, 'You don't have to. Please, let me,' which is a load of bullshit because anyone who's taking out my girl had better buy her a nice meal—and then he's going to tell you your money's no good. That's three."

"Dad, are you sure about this?"

"Is the sky blue? Is the grass green?"

"I don't know. It sounds really complicated."

"Life is complicated, Rowan. Now, pull my finger."

"Dad! You're so gross!"

"Come on, come on—before it goes."

"You're so weird," I said, obliging him.

We both laughed as the fart made its way out, and disappeared into the kitchen. I didn't know getting Mom's permission to go out after the dance would be the least of my problems.

* * *

Despite being an exemplary college preparatory school on the North Shore of Long Island, the Academy had sent a letter home after the hallways were taken over by speculations regarding Kristen Yacendia's custom gown two weeks before the Sadie Hawkins Dance. Apparently, Badgley Mischka was a friend. Either way, Mercy let it be known it would not permit any "attire that contributes to social and economic division among its young women."

"Did you see this crap?" Valentina huffed, slamming her binder onto my lunch tray.

"Dude—my fries! Watch it!"

"This place sucks—it's like we can't do anything."

"What is your deal?"

She laughed at my ignorance, and passed me an envelope. As I removed and unfolded its contents, my eyes grew wider, my temperature hotter.

"Are they serious?" I mumbled, my mouth full of fries.

"I know!" she said, snatching the notice from me. "Check this out: *Excessive cleavage is not allowed*. Looks like you don't have to worry about that one," Valentina laughed, giving my chest a quick pat.

"Shut up, lesbo," I laughed, swatting her hand away. "*No backless, no midriffs*, blah, blah, blah . . . What?! *Dresses may not be above the knee and are not to exceed tea-length. Absolutely no gowns are permitted.* What the hell is tea-length?"

"I don't know, dude."

"Oh my god," I sighed, lowering my head to the table. "My mom's going to kill me—she already got me a dress."

"The red one?"

"Yeah!"

"Well, maybe you can wear it to prom next year."

"That doesn't help me now, though. The red one was, like, a hundred dollars and now she has to buy me another one? Oh my god, my life is over."

On the bus ride home, I wondered how I was going to convince Mom to not only take me to the mall after a full day of watching kids, but also to spend the money she'd earned on yet another dress.

Walking up the driveway, I felt defeated. By the time I reached the back door and kicked off my Oxfords, I'd convinced myself to tell Mom and Cole the dance had been canceled to save myself inevitable disappointment.

"What's with the long face, Smedley?" Dad asked, dangling turkey above his mouth.

"Nothing," I lied, leaning against the fridge.

"Come on. What's bugging you?"

"School gave us this letter that says I need a new dress for the dance."

He laughed at me. "You're getting real crafty about getting to the mall, huh?"

"I'm not lying, Dad! Here, look!" I dug the letter out of my bag and handed it to him.

"Okay, okay. Let's take a look here," he said, carefully scanning the document. "Yeah, that's what I thought. There's nothing on this paper that says, *Rowan Kelly needs a new dress.*"

"Dad!"

"You have a million dresses in that closet of yours—"

"None of those fit me, Dad!"

"All one million of the dresses in your closet don't fit you?"

"Dad, there aren't—"

"Oh yes, yes there are. If we go up there right now, I bet we would count exactly one million dresses."

"Dad!"

"Come on, give me a smile! You're so serious!"

"What's all the yelling about?" Mom said, coming in to fill the kettle for her afternoon tea.

"Nothing," I mumbled.

"How was scho—Joseph Kelly! What are you eating?"

"Not eating," he said slyly, "just munching."

"Well, munch over the sink, you're making a mess," she instructed, giving his arm a loving nudge as he made space for her to pass by. "Rowan, how was school?"

"Okay, I guess." I was still trying to form the question. "Mom?"

"Yes?"

"Can you take me to the mall later? I need to get a new dress for the dance."

"Don't you have a dress upstairs? The red one?" The calm tone of her voice was not surprising. She had been listening. She was always listening.

"Yeah, but—"

"Why do you need a new one if you have a perfectly good one up—"

"Because the school said so!" I snatched the envelope from Dad's hand and waved it in her face. "Gowns aren't allowed anymore."

She took the letter, alternating her gaze between me and the text. I could tell she was trying to work out whether or not I had forged it. Mom knew all my tricks. It never occurred to me they might have been hers once.

"Well," she glanced at the time on the microwave, "I don't know when—"

"I can take her, Mar—"

"No, it has to be Mom!"

The comment took all of us by surprise. I watched Mom soften as she failed to suppress a smile.

"I want to go with *you*, Mom. You know what looks best on me. Please?"

She agreed to take me after the twins left at seven p.m. "If we don't find anything, Dad can watch the kids tomorrow and we'll head over to the Field when you get off the bus. Now, go change and set the table while I get dinner started."

As I ran up the stairs, I rejoiced in knowing I wasn't going to have to cancel on Cole after all. I was grateful Mom had the money, the time, the patience.

It seemed every time my eyes looked to the clock located above the chalkboard, it read 2:17 p.m. Where was Sister Monica with the announcements? Wasn't the day over? As the second hand ticked along, and I hardened my stare hoping to accelerate time, Valentina brushed my shoulder.

What? I mouthed, not wanting to catch Mr. D'Amico's attention.

Valentina scribbled on her notebook and pushed it to the edge of her desk. After a quick glance to the front of the classroom, I leaned over.

"Excited?"

I couldn't suppress the smile and nodded.

"What color is your dress again?"

"Black," I whispered, "and it's got these—"

"Um, ladies? Is there something you would like to share with the rest of us?"

"No," we both giggled.

"Well, uh, let's try to stay focused here, girls. This stuff's going to be on the Regents so let's get back to it. Now, which property is used to determine the degree of polarity between two bonded atoms?"

As Mr. D'Amico droned on about the difference between density, pressure, temperature, and electronegativity, I thought about my dress. It extended just below my knees, the straight across neckline was held up by spaghetti straps, and it had an empire waist. While I had originally wanted the lavender, Mom made me try on the black in the fitting room, knowing it was the right choice. With a silver glitter overlay, the dress seemed to sparkle.

"Do you like it?" I asked Mom when I'd tried it on.

"I don't have to like it. You're the one who has to wear it. Do *you* like it?"

Hyper-aware Mom was watching the mirror; I withheld an eye roll. Why couldn't she just tell me I looked nice? Why couldn't she say the dress was perfect?

"I guess it's okay."

"If you don't like it then take it off, and let's go out there and find something you do like."

"I just, I don't *know* if I like it or not."

"Well, how do you feel? Can you move in it?"

"Yeah," I said, swaying back and forth.

"I think it fits you very well."

"Really?"

It was always this way between us—me asking a question, Mom unwilling to provide a straight answer. I hated how Mom never appeared to care about anything important to me, how I wasn't worthy of her opinion. It was years before I realized she was teaching me how to discover myself, to know my own mind, to be unapologetically me.

"I love it."

"Good—now take it off. If you hurry, we might be able to grab a pretzel before we go."

"Good afternoon, ladies," Sister Monica's voice crackled through the loudspeaker. *"May I have your attention please?"*

The class shared a sigh of relief—we'd survived the day. All that was left was to go home, get ready, and hope tonight was the night our dreams and fantasies about falling in love came true.

The school bus had barely rounded the corner of Elderberry before I was out of my seat and down the aisle.

"Please," our bus driver Vinny said, extending his right arm before me, while keeping his left on the steering wheel, "please remain behind the white line."

I leaped off the bus before it had a chance to come to a complete stop and sprinted toward our house. Jogging up the driveway, I spotted Dad's head through the kitchen window. Upon entering the kitchen, I found him eating part of last night's ham steak over the sink, and I began to whine.

"I'll do it," he said.

"When?"

"When I do it."

"When is that going to be?"

"Rowan, please—all right? I just got in. Can I get two minutes without anybody bothering me?"

"But Cole is going to be here soon. How am I going to know he's here if the doorbell doesn't work?"

My concern wasn't so much needing to know when Cole arrived, but was born out of a desperate need to prevent Mom from getting to him before I could. With the doorbell to warn me, I could clear the hallway, the stairs, and the living room by the time Mom had stopped whatever she was doing in the kitchen. If Mom got there first, though, who knew what embarrassing things she would say to him in the time it took me to run down the hallway, jump down the stairs, and across the fancy couches we weren't allowed to put our feet on?

"Well, I assume he knows how to knock."

"Dad, if you don't fix the doorbell, I'll, I'll . . ." Tears were already spilling out of my eyes and onto the kitchen floor before I could think of a consequence severe enough to force Dad to bend to my will.

"Oh, come on," he laughed, opening his arms for a hug.

"No," I said, pushing him away. "No. Get away!"

"Don't be so dramatic!" He smiled, arms still open.

"Are you going to fix it or not?"

"Yes," he laughed, "I'm going to fix it."

"Do you promise?"

"I promise. Now come give your father a hug."

I relented and stepped forward so he could squeeze me. Dad always had a way of pulling tight when he hugged, as if he was afraid of losing us.

"Okay," I said, trying to catch my breath from blubbering, "but, like, *when* are you going to fix it?"

After my talk with Dad, I raced everywhere—up the stairs

to lay out my dress, to the bathroom to do my hair, down the hall so Mom could do my makeup.

Mom sat me in a chair at the kitchen table for better lighting—her red, quilted makeup bag between us. She pulled out a slim pink tube with a green tip and told me to look up.

"What's this?"

"Mascara," she said softly, concentrating on the application.

"It feels funny."

"I'm surprised you can feel it," she laughed. "You barely have any lashes." She put the brush back in the bottle and shook it furiously.

"I want to see!" I rushed down the hall to the bathroom, hit the light, and stood close to the mirror. "They don't look different!" I called back to her.

"Well, come back here—I'm not done yet!"

As I dropped back into the chair, I began to look at her—like, really look at her. Mom's eyelashes extended past her eyelids, clearly visible. Her eyes were round and blue, like marbles, and popped against her blue-tinted lashes.

"Why do your eyelashes look blue?" I asked, noticing this for the first time.

"Because," she laughed.

"Because why?"

"Because, Rowan—hold still!" she hissed. I closed my mouth when the tip of her tongue crept out of the corner of hers, signifying she was not to be interrupted. After a moment, she added, "I use blue-tinted mascara because my eyes are blue and it brings them out. Now, look up."

"Why can't you do the blue on mine, like yours?"

"You have brown eyes so the black is going to make them look fuller and more noticeable. Now, please. Look. Up."

She gave me a smoky eye and a pink lip. "Beautiful. Make sure not to kiss Cole or you'll mess it up," she chuckled.

"Mom!"

The doorbell echoed through the house, and I began to sweat at an alarming rate. As I sprinted to open the door, I realized how grossly unprepared I was for this entire evening—what would we talk about? What if he didn't dance? What if Mom pulled out the photo album?

"Whoa." Cole smiled as I opened the door.

"Hey!"

"Hey," he said, looking me up and down. "You look—"

"Thanks!" I said, checking over my shoulder. I'd strategically left the tickets and my purse on the table by the door so I could make a quick exit. "You ready?"

"Yeah, but I figured I'd say hi to your parents—"

"Oh no, you don't need to do that." I hurriedly tried to close the door behind me when I heard Mom.

"Rowan! Is that Cole?" It wasn't a question—she already knew the answer.

I bowed my head in defeat—there was no escape. The sound of her shoes pierced through the living room as Cole entered my home.

"Hi, I'm Marie—Rowan's mom." She smiled, extending her hand for a shake. "You must be Cole. It's so nice of you to take Rowan to the dance."

"It's nice of her to ask me."

"Would you mind just a few pictures by the fireplace?"

"Of course not!"

The camera appeared as if from nowhere, but Cole never seemed uncomfortable. He put his arm around me and smiled as flash after flash blinded us. I was grateful Mom didn't ask us to hold hands, fearing he wouldn't want to.

"Is this Cole?" Dad asked, strolling into the living room as the photo shoot was ending. "Hi, Joe Kelly—nice to meet you."

"Hi, Mr. Kelly."

"Oh please—Joe is fine. So, all set for the big date?"

"It's not a date!" I screamed. "It's a dance, Dad."

"Yeah, but he's your date, isn't he?"

Cole laughed nervously. We hadn't discussed if this was a date or not. We hadn't discussed if we were dating . . . we hadn't discussed anything.

"Dad," I said through gritted teeth.

"So, Cole—Rowan tells us you go to Nassau Community. What are you studying there?" Mom asked, changing the subject.

"I don't really have a major," he responded confidently. "I'm taking a couple of different classes and seeing what interests me."

"That's the way to do it," Dad said. "And you work too?"

"Yeah, I've been working at Journey's for, like, two years now."

"Very good, very good."

"Have fun!" Mom said, still smiling.

Dad ushered us out the door and closed it behind us. We'd survived.

"Dude, I am so sorry about my parents. They're so weird!" I said, walking down the front path to the sidewalk where his car was parked.

"It's no problem," he laughed. "I was kind of expecting it."

"Really?"

"Well, yeah, I am, like, way older than you."

"Three years doesn't make you *way* older."

"To parents it does." He quickened his pace as we walked toward his green Buick. He inserted the key and opened the passenger door with a bow. "Madame."

"Thank you, good sir."

The seat cushions were soft and blue, and smelled of weed and McDonald's. E-Z Wider rolling papers and bottles of Mountain Dew covered the car floor, but I managed to find a place to put my feet.

"Sorry it's a mess in here," he said, tossing some bottles into the backseat.

"It's cool." I meant it.

My right hand ran alongside the door, up along the window, searching for the seat belt. I pulled it across my dress, and fumbled for the buckle.

"Having some trouble there?" he asked, hitting the light above us.

"Thanks," I replied, finally clicking the buckle in place as I noticed his gaze. "What?"

"Nothing," he laughed. "I just can't get over how different you look."

I smiled. "*Good* different?"

"I don't know," he said. "I guess, it's just—"

"Just what?"

"It's just that you don't look like *you*."

"I look that different?" I asked, pulling down the visor.

My lips were hot pink and looked as if I'd smeared butter all over them. The Juicy Tube in my bag was just in case the shine wore off later in the evening. My cheeks had a subtle layer of blush—enough not to be misconstrued as a temperature, enough for people who saw me daily to know something was different.

The eye shadow was a blush smoky eye with pink glitter in the corners of my eyes. Mom had done a great job copying the look I'd seen in *Cosmo Girl*. I thought the makeup made me look older, sophisticated . . . pretty.

"Don't worry about it," he said, putting the car in drive. "You look great."

"Do you have any water or anything?"

"Nah, but I can stop somewhere if you want."

"Yeah, there's a 7-Eleven at the intersection if you make a left."

"Cool."

I asked the cashier for the bathroom key, but was told there was no key, that someone must be in there. I let five minutes pass before I purchased a large Fiji water and snatched some napkins.

"Got what you need?"

"Yeah," I said, leaving my door open.

I placed several napkins in my hand and poured on the water. Once successfully damp, I began scrubbing my face.

"What are you doing?" he laughed. "You're crazy!"

The napkins in my lap were different shades of pink with patches of glitter, and occasional streaks of black from the mascara. As the water ran low, the pink faded until all that was left were wet napkins.

"Better?" I said, turning to Cole.

"Yeah," he smiled. "You look like you now. You don't need all that shit. How about some tunes?"

"Sure, whaddaya got?"

"Underneath the seat," he said, pulling out of the 7-Eleven parking lot.

I reached under and pulled out the same Case Logic binder I used to keep all my CDs together. Unlike mine, though, I'd never heard of these bands—The Cure, Joy Division, Sonic Youth.

"Who are The Smiths?"

"Who are The Smiths? Who *are* The Smiths?! Give me that!" He began pawing at the CDs with his right hand, trying to steer with his left.

"Here," I said, pulling a black CD from the sleeve. "I got it."

Cole pushed the forward button eight times, and the music came on: *Take me out tonight . . .*

"What's this song called?"

"Shhh," he said, "just listen."

Take me out tonight
Where there's music and there's people
And they're young and alive
Driving in your car
I never, never want to go home
Because I haven't got one anymore . . .

"Why does he sound so sad?"

"You think he sounds sad?"

"Kind of," I laughed.

"No, he's not sad," Cole smiled. "I think he's, like, re-

ally really happy. Like he's riding with this girl and everything is just, like, perfect, and he doesn't need anything
else, you know?"

"Yeah, I get that."

"So, this is where you go to school?" he asked, putting
the car in park.

"Yeah, this is it."

"Cool."

Cole shoved his hands in his pockets, looking around
anxiously. I couldn't tell if it was nerves or if he was looking for a way out.

"Do you want to go inside?"

"Yeah, sure."

He walked around the car, clicked his heels to attention, and extended his right arm. I looped my left through,
and we began to walk.

"Are those—are those bars on the windows?"

"Yup."

"Are they trying to keep people out or keep you
guys in?"

"Not sure—probably a little bit of both. Apparently,
it was a school during a war or something. My grandma
was, like, one of the first people to go here."

"That's pretty cool."

"Really? I always thought it was kind of lame."

As we approached the double doors leading to the
auditorium, my eyes met Sister Margaret Anne's. I'd been
in her office for smoking in the bathroom two weeks
prior, and last month for forging Mom's signature on a
note Sister Joan sent home about my "attitude."

Sister Margaret Anne had a permanent wrinkle above

her nose from being in a constant state of trying to sniff out bullshit. She was shaped like an apple between the neckline and the knee, and was born with a bowl cut.

"Good evening, Rowan," she said as we came up to the door. She had a way of making everything sound like an accusation.

"Hi, Sister Margaret Anne," I mumbled, surrendering my tickets.

"And who is this young man with you tonight?"

"Hi, my name is Cole," he said, putting his hand forward.

I imagine she had a firm grip because Cole's back stiffened as she shook it. "Well, you two have a good—excuse me," she said, holding her arm out to stop us from going forward. "What are those?"

Our eyes followed her finger to the floor. Cole's feet were covered by black and white–checkered slip-ons.

"Oh," he smiled, unfamiliar with the peril usually following Sister Margaret Anne's tone, "they're Vans."

"And what are Vans?"

"They're sneakers," he said, trying not to laugh.

"Young man," she said, coming closer to us, "this is a formal dance for the young ladies. These *Vans* are entirely inappropriate and against the dress code. I—" I'm not sure if it was the line forming behind us, or the look of despair on my face, but Sister Margaret Anne seemed to stop herself before, what I assume, was going to be a dismissal. "Perhaps be more mindful next time, Miss Kelly. In you go."

"Jesus," Cole said once we were inside, letting go of a deep breath. "My life just flashed before my eyes."

"Yeah, she's insane."

We found Valentina in the middle of the dance floor and laughed about how many expletives the DJ was forced to bleep out. Then the room got quiet, and the DJ spoke. "All right, Mercy girls, how you all doing tonight?"

The auditorium gave a big "woo" as we threw our hands in the air.

"Right on! That's what I like to hear," he said. "Now this is a dance, so I want you to grab your man's hand, make him put his arms around you, and sway to this one."

The auditorium giggled with the laughter of 150 teenage girls being granted permission to get close to the opposite gender. Couples moved to the center as those without dates retreated to the borders of the dance floor.

Unlike Dad, Cole simply placed both hands on my hips, pulled me in close, and began swaying from side to side.

If you're not the one then why does my soul feel glad today?
If you're not the one then why does my hand fit yours this way?

"Man," he laughed, "what is this?"

"I don't know," I lied, "but it's *bad*." I continued to sing Daniel Bedingfield's latest single—which I was determined to play as the first dance with my future husband—in my head.

"Seriously, the music nowadays is such shit."

"Hey, there are good bands, okay?"

"Like who?"

"Like, um, Radiohead and No Doubt . . . Blink 182?"

"Okay, I'll give you Radiohead, but the other two—I don't know."

"Just dance," I laughed.

He smiled and took a step closer, letting me rest my head on his chest. I'd known Cole a little more than a year. At first, he was Chris's friend. In the past several months, he'd evolved into a boy I'd make out with on occasion. But on that dance floor, for a breath, I got a glimpse of someone else—a man I'd yet to know, but wanted to . . . a man I wanted to know me.

"Excuse me," Sister Margaret Anne interrupted, placing her hand on my shoulder, and a ruler on Cole's. We each took a step backward as the sister wedged the ruler between us horizontally and said, "Let's leave room for the Holy Spirit, shall we?" before moving on to the next couple.

Cole and I bowed our heads when she was out of sight and let the laughter go.

"Dude," he said, "she *is* crazy!"

"I know!"

Our snickers turned to silence, and I recognized I liked Cole. Not just liked, but like-liked. I was convinced he could make everything okay . . . that he could make *me* okay.

"Aw man," sighed the DJ as the song faded away, "I wish y'all could see how beautiful you look tonight. And while I wish we could take it slow the rest of the night, a little birdie told me y'all are here to party . . . Are you ready to party?" he howled, more like a proclamation than a question. We screamed yes—yes, we were here to party. But he already knew. "Okay, let's party!"

People came back to the floor and we were surrounded.

They were bumping and shoving and knocking into us as I tried frantically to hold onto whatever was happening inside me.

"Hey," Cole shouted, shimmying his way back to me, "you wanna get out of here?"

"Yeah."

"Okay, let's go."

The brisk, almost-April evening stole the air from my lungs and left me gasping for breath as we walked back to the Buick.

"Where should we go?" he asked.

The time glowed green through the darkness—9:32 p.m. We had all the time in the world.

"Anywhere."

"Cool, pick another CD," he said, putting the car in drive and peeling out of the parking lot.

"All these bands start with 'The': The Clash, The Cure—is it like a requirement or something?"

"No," he smirked, "it's like an indicator of greatness. All great bands start with 'The'—The Beatles, The Who—"

"The Backstreet Boys?"

Silence.

"Ha! I got you."

"Yeah, yeah. Well, you won't find any Backstreet Boys CDs in there, so pick one."

I flipped through pages and pages of CDs before a dark cover with a pale man's face looked up at me. "*Disintegration*," I read.

"Oh yeah, that's a good one. Skip to track two—you're going to like that one."

A hint of sea salt crept through the vents, and I realized we were on Ocean Parkway, headed for Jones Beach.

There was nothing particularly special about Jones Beach—the water wasn't clear enough to see straight down to your toes, the sand wasn't so fine it felt more like sugar, and the boardwalk wasn't lined with souvenir T-shirt shops—yet it was magical.

Most people don't know Jones Beach is actually on Jones Beach Island, sandwiched between Long Beach and Fire Island. To get to it, you have to take the highway—either the Meadowbrook or the Wantagh—all the way down and then over a bridge or two until it turns into Ocean Parkway.

The lights and sounds and traffic of Long Island disappear and are replaced with this feeling that anything can happen. Not because it's nighttime and not because it's the beach, but because it's the one place where the world gets quiet. That's why every Long Island native loves Jones Beach.

Cole pulled into the middle of two parking spaces in Parking Field 4, rolled the windows down, and turned the volume up.

"Come on," he said, getting out of the car.

I unclicked my seat belt and followed him back toward the trunk. Cole tossed the jumper cables aside and tucked a towel under his arm. We walked around to the front of the car and he told me not to laugh as he rolled a faded Power Rangers towel over the windshield.

The hood was hot against my dress, which balanced out the cool ocean breeze coming in and out with the Jones Beach waves. We were lying on the hood as *Disintegration* started over. Cole sat up and reached into his pocket, pulling out a round, silver cylinder no taller than his thumb.

"You ever smoke before?"

"No," I said, wishing I'd lied.

"You wanna try?"

"Yeah," I smiled, sitting up.

Cole twisted the grinder as he surveyed the area for law enforcement and set it down between us. In his jacket pocket, he removed a box of E-Z Wider. He took a sheet and began making small accordion folds at each end before filling the paper with the grinder's contents. Cole then rolled the paper back and forth, licked the ends, and sealed it.

"You ever smoke, like, a cigarette or anything?" he asked, turning to me.

"Nope," I said, adjusting myself to face him.

I watched as he pushed each end of the joint in and out of his mouth before running his lighter along it horizontally.

"Okay," he said, lighting the end of the joint, "you're going to take a deep breath in." He inhaled, with me following suit.

"And let it out." He exhaled, and put the joint between his lips. "Then you're gonna inhale, hold it," he instructed through clenched teeth, "count to three, then," he let out another breath, and smoke along with it. I watched as he repeated the procedure, knowing I was definitely going to fuck it up.

"Now you try," he said, passing the joint to me.

I rested the joint on my lower lip and immediately coughed as the smoke made its way up my nose. He laughed as I continued to cough and took the joint back.

"Here. Wrap your pinky around mine—got it? Okay, now widen your fingers a little bit." We assumed the pinky-promise position, and for a moment I thought we were going to exchange secrets like lovers did. Instead, Cole showed me how to form a tunnel, pressing the edges of our pinkies together. "Good—I'm going to blow smoke through and all you have to do is breathe, hold it, and let it go. You ready?"

"Ready," I said.

The smoke came through fast and I inhaled deeply, trying to catch it. I let it fill my mouth and tried to hold on as tears welled in my eyes and the cough escaped my chest.

"That's it," he said, patting me on the back, "cough it out."

"Did I do it right?"

"Yeah—one more time, though. I don't know how much you got," he said, raising his pinky again.

"You feel it yet?" he asked after a few minutes.

"Yeah," I lied, "totally."

"Can't tell, huh?"

"Not even a little bit."

We'd whittled the joint down to a little more than half an inch. Most of the time, I just inhaled, held the smoke between my cheeks, and puffed it out.

"Okay, this is going to come really fast." Cole sat up and told me to face him. "When the smoke comes out, suck in as much as you can. You ready?"

I nodded and braced myself as Cole inhaled deeply and stuck the lit end of the joint into his mouth, clenching what remained of it with his teeth. He folded his lips over it and cupped my chin with his hand, guiding me toward him and placing my lips around the joint. Then he exhaled. The smoke came quick and hot as I pulled it into my mouth.

My eyes began to water, and my throat burned as the smoke snaked its way into my lungs. The cough was worse than before. Cole flicked the roach away and kept telling me to "cough to get off." Eventually, the cough faded, and I lay down beside him.

I felt the condensation from the hood of the car coming through my skin, into my blood. The sea salt in the air danced on my body as the streetlights from the parking lot grew brighter, blurrier.

I held my arms above me to see my hands, and waved them back and forth, giggling as they moved through the air, leaving parts of themselves behind. Cole snatched one and kissed it.

His lips traveled from my palm up my arm, tickling my neck. "Kiss me."

"You were right," I said, when we finally stopped kissing and lay back again, gazing up at the stars. "I do really like this song."

"Told you."

"How'd you get into their music?"

"Tom introduced me to them."

"Who's Tom?"

"He's my best friend. Well, he was. He killed himself last year."

"What?"

"Yeah."

"I'm so sorry," I said, reaching toward him.

"It's fine," he said, shaking off my hand. "I don't really talk about it."

At fifteen, I hadn't known anyone who'd died, let alone anyone who had taken their own life. Death had always seemed so far away. I was desperate to be older—able to move out, to drink, to live. And yet, Tom had chosen to die. I wondered what had happened.

The *whoop-whoop* of a state trooper cruiser pierced through "Lullaby." I saw red and blue lights flashing across my dress. I was suddenly aware I was alive—that the reason the trooper was here was because the booming of my heart must have been disturbing everyone within a hundred-mile radius. It dawned on me I was also about to be thrown in jail. I'd committed a crime—I'd used an illegal substance. Mom was going to be pissed.

Cole turned to me, seemingly unphased, put his hand on my hand, and whispered, "Be cool."

Inherently uncool, I panicked and doubted my ability to act cool now that I was about to be facing three-to-five.

"Evening, officer," Cole said, sliding off the hood.

"You kids aware this area is closed?" the trooper responded flatly.

"I'm sorry about that. We were just hanging out."

"Hanging out?" the trooper repeated, shining his flashlight in my eyes. "Anything else going on here?" he asked, surveying the area.

Cole nodded and continued, "We were just heading out. Sorry, officer."

The trooper inched closer, no doubt moving toward the thumping of my heart, which I was certain had started to come through my ribs and out my chest.

"You kids look all dressed up."

"We just came from a dance," Cole said, stepping back to maintain distance from the man who was about to put us in the slammer. Did people even call it "the slammer"?

"How about you get her home?" he said, shining the

light in Cole's eyes. "It's late. And, like I said, this area is closed."

"Again, really sorry about that, officer."

"Don't let it happen again. Drive safe."

Cole walked back to me, gave me a thumbs-up, and gestured for me to get back in the car. My palms squeaked as I slid off the hood and scurried back into the Buick, heart still pounding.

After the trooper drove off, Cole and I shared a look and began to laugh. We laughed until our stomachs reached our spines and the air had gone from our lungs. Our eyes watered and our hands clapped together until we came to.

"You hungry?" he asked.

"Yeah. I'm starved."

"I'll have waffle fries with mozzarella cheese, no gravy, and a Coke, please," I said, handing my menu over.

"We don't have Coke, we have Pepsi—is that okay?"

"Yeah, sure."

"And for you, sweetheart?"

"Can I get the short stack of pancakes and a side of sausage?"

"Anything to drink?"

"A chocolate milkshake—no whipped cream, though."

"Coming right up."

She walked away with our menus and Cole turned back toward me, asking if I was upset about leaving the dance early.

"No way."

"Okay, cool. It just isn't my scene, and honestly, I was getting a little weirded out."

"Really? Why?"

"I don't know. I guess it's just that you're so young—"

"Oh my god, I'm not *that* young," I laughed. "You, like, just graduated."

"Last year, but . . ."

"But what?"

"It'd be different if you were a senior or something. Then maybe we could—never mind."

"Then we could what?"

"Nothing, forget it."

The waitress set the faux-leather check presenter between us after the plates had been cleared. I went to grab it, as Dad had instructed. I had just slipped my fingers underneath and was lifting it upward when Cole laughed and said, "Hey, what are you doing? Gimme that."

He opened the check presenter, then his wallet. As he thumbed through fives and singles, I reached into my purse.

"Hey, put your money away!" *That's two.*

"Are you sure?"

"Yeah," he smiled, slipping two twenties into the plastic flap and closing it. "I got it. You ready?"

Cole opened the door for me to exit, and I started to understand what he'd meant about the three-year gap between us. More than just years separated us. I couldn't drive, I couldn't vote, I couldn't drink. We, and whatever was between us, could only exist in the Journey's stock room.

"Do you like me?"

"Of course I like you. I wouldn't hang out with you if I didn't like you."

"Would you ever, like, date me?"

"I—I don't know."

"Because I'm not old enough?"

"Well, yeah! And you're my best friend's cousin, and you're probably going to be going to college soon, and—"

"So? I could go to college here."

"That's not the point."

"Then what is the point?"

"Look, you're a cool chick and I like you, but you're always going to be Chris's little cousin."

"Yeah, I guess so."

"And I'm sure your parents wouldn't be cool with it. Your mom didn't seem to think me not having a major was a great idea."

"Yeah," I said. *Why did Mom have to ask so many stupid questions?*

"Are you okay?"

"Yeah. I'm good."

After Cole started the car, I was convinced the clock was wrong—there was no way it could be 12:13 a.m. I slouched in my seat—the night had been a waste. We'd barely danced two slow songs, gotten in trouble with Sister Margaret Anne, Cole wasn't going to be my boyfriend, and I'd missed curfew.

Maybe it was because another hour wasn't going to change anything. Maybe it was because I felt the night owed me more than two slow dances and glassy eyes. But really, I just wanted to prove I wasn't a kid.

"Hey, put your seat belt on," Cole commanded, looking to make sure no one was behind us.

Instead of a center console, the Buick had a seat between the driver and the passenger. I slid myself across, into the nook between Cole's bicep and underarm.

"Wait," I said.

He put the car in park and let me kiss him. Between kisses, I opened my eyes to see the windows had begun to fog. I decided this was my chance and straddled him. I didn't stop his hands from fondling my breasts, squeezing my ass.

I could feel his penis begin to harden and placed my hand on it.

"Wait," he said. "Wait a second."

The more I touched it, the harder it became.

"Rowan," he said. "Rowan!"

"It's okay," I assured him.

"Wait!" he said angrily, firmly placing his hands on my hips, and relocating me to the middle seat. "I can't do this."

"Why?"

He didn't answer me. He didn't look at me as he turned on the defroster and rolled the windows down.

When we pulled up to the house on Elderberry, the light from my parents' bedroom went on instantly.

Cole walked around to my side of the car and opened the door. We walked side by side up the path to the front door, lights flicking on as we approached.

"Are you in trouble or something?"

"Yeah . . . probably."

"Look, I'm really sorry about that thing in the car earlier."

"It's okay."

He gave me a quick peck on the lips, thanked me for the invite, and told me he'd see me around. I watched his tall, slim silhouette move down toward the sidewalk, unaware of how he'd continue to walk away in the coming months.

"Rowan Joy Kelly," Mom called from the back door. I knew I was doomed when she used my full name. "Get. In. Here. Now."

Mom stepped into the driveway, setting off the sensor. Under the spotlight, she stood arms crossed against her chest, wearing the red terry-cloth bathrobe and matching slippers I'd gotten her last Christmas. She'd stopped coloring her hair in the summer. Naturally, she had been a blonde, but her roots had gotten dark and given way to grays, which seemed to shimmer under the light.

As I walked toward her, I thought of all the excuses I could use—we lost track of time, the waitress wouldn't give us our check, Valentina's date needed a ride home—when it occurred to me this was all *her* fault. It was Mom who asked about Nassau, it was Mom who gave me a curfew . . . it was Mom who set all these dumb rules about dating. It was Mom who'd gotten in the way of Cole wanting to date me, and I was going to make her pay for it.

When I reached her, I turned to go up the stairs, only for her to block my path. "Do you have any idea what time it is?"

"I don't know," I sighed. "You wouldn't buy me a Baby-G watch so—"

She grabbed my arm, her nails digging into my skin, and pulled me up the stairs before hurling me into the laundry room and slamming the door behind her, shaking rolls of paper towels off the shelves.

"What did you say to me?"

"What are you, deaf?"

"IT IS ONE O'CLOCK IN THE GODDAMN

MORNING!" she screamed, following me into the kitchen. I'd decided I wasn't going to fight her—I was going upstairs to bed. "YOU WERE SUPPOSED TO BE HOME AT ELEVEN O'CLOCK!"

"Actually," I said, turning and pointing to the clock above our kitchen table, "it's 12:53 in the morning."

Mom charged me and banged her hands against the table again and again. "I DON'T GIVE A SHIT WHAT TIME IT IS—"

"THEN WHY ARE YOU YELLING AT ME ABOUT IT?!" I shouted back.

"BECAUSE YOU WERE SUPPOSED TO BE HOME TWO GODDAMN HOURS AGO AND I'VE BEEN— I'VE BEEN . . ." The top part of her body collapsed onto the table, her bottom half still holding a firm stance, and she began to cry. The entirety of her body began shaking, as if her rage had reached its maximum and was trying to make its way out. Her sobs were guttural, the volume and intensity of her screams were starting to catch up with her. I went to touch her, and she snapped back, her finger pointed in my direction. "I HAVE BEEN UP, WORRIED SICK—SICK TO MY GODDAMN STOMACH, ROWAN!"

Dad shuffled into the kitchen and went to put his arms around Mom. I didn't know if he'd been watching us the whole time or if he'd been awakened by our fight. "Rowan," he said, shaking his head, "your mother's right. You were supposed to be home at eleven p.m., it's now one in the morning. Where were you?"

"None of your business," I snapped.

"Oh," Dad laughed, "yes, it is my business. You're my daughter, you live in my house, you are my business."

"It doesn't matter," Mom said, placing her hand over her heart, "because whatever she says won't be the truth. Isn't that right, Rowan?"

I said nothing.

"She doesn't know how to tell the truth. Everything out of her mouth is a lie."

"Then why are you asking me?" I laughed.

"DON'T YOU LAUGH AT ME!" she said, pushing past Dad and coming right to my nose. "BECAUSE I AM YOUR MOTHER! I AM YOUR MOTHER, ROWAN, AND I HAVE A RIGHT TO KNOW WHERE YOU WERE, GODDAMNIT!"

"We were with Valentina at the diner and—"

"Oh no," she laughed. "Stop, just stop, okay? Valentina has been home since midnight. See? Do you even know how to tell the truth? Seriously, do you?"

"Yes," I spat back.

"Oh yeah? Let's go down the list. You tell me you're going somewhere, and then Mrs. Kirk catches you at the movies with a boy—"

"YOU WOULDN'T LET ME GO IF I TOLD YOU WHERE I WAS GOING—"

"BECAUSE THERE ARE RULES IN THIS HOUSE AND YOU DON'T NEED TO BE GOING TO MOVIE THEATERS WITH BOYS!"

"What are you so afraid of? That I'm going to get pregnant? I'm not stupid, Mom!"

"THAT'S NOT THE POINT!" she shrieked, tears streaming down her face, snot bubbling from her nose. "THAT IS NOT THE GODDAMN POINT! You are my daughter, I—I . . ." She took a seat on the bench and sank her head into her palms.

Dad rubbed her back and tried to soothe her: "Okay, okay, shhh. I think it's time we all go to bed. Rowan, we'll talk about this in the morning."

Mom perked her head up and added, "You are done for the weekend, you understand? No phone, no TV, no stereo, no mall—nothing. You hear me? NOTHING! You will not leave this house for three months. THREE MONTHS!"

"I hate you," I said plainly.

"Oh yeah?" she said, wiping tears away. "Well, I love you. Because that's what mothers do."

"Then I wish you weren't my mother," I said, marching up the stairs.

As I lay awake in bed that night, I listened to Mom's sobs from down the hall. I didn't know the dark places her mind had gone to before I came home—how she feared me beaten, raped, left for dead. How she thought back to my first steps, the first time I called her "Mama," the look on my face on Christmas morning. I didn't know a mother's greatest fear is her child never coming home. I didn't know there'd be nights where I'd be wishing to be in my room, in the house on Elderberry, safe and sound with Mom down the hall.

CHAPTER FIVE

"YOU KNOW," NURSE SIGHS as she marks my measurements in my file, "I always wanted to adopt."

"Oh yeah?"

"Yeah," she smiles. "I'm an only child, and always wished I had an older brother or a little sister. And now I have an only child."

Nurse reaches into her breast pocket, and hands me a photo. Her long braids are tucked under a light-blue scrub cap, beads of sweat across her forehead. The baby in her arms is red from screaming, wrapped in a blue blanket.

"How old—"

"He's nineteen months this Tuesday," she smiles, slipping him back into her pocket. "There were complications, so I can't carry again. But I want him to have someone to play with, you know?"

I nod. "I always wanted a sister."

"Me too!" Nurse laughs, lightly tapping my shoulder. "I always wanted to adopt a little Asian girl so I could dress her up like Boo from *Monsters, Inc.* You know Boo? Then Evan could be Mike Wazowski! They make these cute little costumes on Etsy."

"Yeah, that'd make a great picture."

* * *

Mom and Dad were from large families—Mom was one of ten, and Dad was one of twelve. Mom's siblings were easy to remember—Charlie, Billy, Danny, Tommy, Corey, Lucy, Maggie, Annie, and Jackie. Dad's were more difficult—Morgan had been in and out of rehab since he tried to smother me with a pillow on a bad acid trip, Sean lived in Seattle, and Deirdre only called on the first of the month to tell Nana she was sober and needed money. And Shane? Well, Shane lived in fucking Malaysia and didn't send shit for Christmas.

I'd always heard the same thing when it came to Uncle Shane—he got a perfect score on his SATs—as if this was an indicator he was not like the rest of the Kellys.

Not only was he the first of them to attend college, he was also the first to leave home. This was the other thing I heard—he went into the Peace Corps, met a woman in Malaysia, and did not return.

As a senior, I'd evolved from PSAT-prep worry to full-blown SAT panic. My scores had come back lower than expected. Mom was surpised I'd chosen to spend the summer studying to retake the exam in the fall. A solid score was my ticket off this island, away from Mom and her rules.

One afternoon, I returned home from Mercy to find a blow-up mattress in the middle of my room. I clenched my fists and stormed down the hallway.

"Mom!" Lately, my tone had more of a why-do-you-fucking-exist flavor, as opposed to I-can't-find-my-socks.

"Yes, Rowan?"

"Why is there a mattress in my room?"

"The real question is: how did your father manage to blow it up with the mess you call your room?"

"What is it doing there?"

"Your Malaysian cousins are coming to visit us for a little while."

"What?" I screamed. "Why do they have to stay in my room? Why can't they stay in Aidan's room?"

"They are. The two boys are staying with Aidan and the girls are staying with you."

"For how long?"

"For however long they're staying. Please, Rowan, go clean your room. I don't want this house to be a mess when they get here."

This was so like her. We'd fought the week before about something, and she'd been ignoring me, all the while plotting her vengeance. Mom graduated valedictorian from the Passive Aggressive Institute of America with an advanced degree in the Silent Treatment. Nothing breaks her. Her MO is to make you sweat out the fight, to get you to crave forgiveness . . . to make you speak first.

Everyone seemed so excited Uncle Shane was returning home with his wife Jovinia and their children: Gerard, James, Danielle, and Michelle. Yet no one actually said Uncle Shane was coming back with his family. They simply referred to all of them as "The Malaysians."

I'd only ever seen them on Nana's fridge. The photo was taken over eight Christmases ago, against the laser-photo background every cool kid chose for their school pictures. The term "The Malaysians" evoked more than a sense of mystery—more than not knowing if they spoke English or if they'd ever seen *Titanic*—it was a distinction. The Kellys I saw at Christmases and whose checks I cashed on or around November 5—they were my real family. We didn't know who The Malaysians were.

The house on Elderberry originally belonged to Dad's mother, whom we called Nana. My grandfather, Rowan James, passed before we had the chance to meet. At his wake, my parents received the call informing them they were approved for the adoption and would be receiving a little girl. It was then they decided to name me Rowan.

Halfway through kindergarten, Nana began to feel the house was too much work for just her. We left the Tudor on Weybridge and moved into the house on Elderberry, where Dad assessed the damage.

Nana was supposed to move in with Fiona, but things fell through after it turned out Fiona's husband was financing a gambling problem, not condos in Florida. Cara said she'd take Nana in, but only until Kerry was born—allowing just enough time for Dad to build an extension on the house on Elderberry.

Dad's default setting was working. On Saturdays, my grandfather would wake him and his eleven siblings early, and use a turntable to play the best of Rodgers and Hammerstein, Sondheim, and Gershwin, while they cleaned the house, tended the yard, and shined shoes for Sunday service. It is for this reason almost every Kelly function ends with a sing-along.

After taking Mom to senior prom, Dad enrolled in trade school and began his apprenticeship as a carpenter. At sixty-four, two years shy of the full benefit, he refers to himself as semi-retired, but there are still many days where he leaves the house before I do to make things with his hands.

As a child, the only time I saw Dad was for Sunday breakfast. Aidan and I would wake to the smell of bacon and rush down the stairs to get first pick of the bagels Dad and Mom had picked up on their way home from church. As Mom poached eggs and fried the corned beef hash, she'd charge us with setting the table—Aidan carried the cream cheese and the butter and I got to carry the orange juice. Sometimes, Mom would get up from the table early and go into the kitchen for a few moments. Minutes later, Aidan and I would get a whiff of the Pillsbury cinnamon rolls and run to the oven to watch them puff up. Once they were out of the oven, we each got a butter knife to spread the icing before licking our fingers clean.

During the week, Dad rose at four a.m. to shower, make tea, and listen to the radio. Once he finished hearing about the Jets' prospects or the weather, he'd climb back up the stairs to lay a kiss on our foreheads before lacing up his Timberlands and walking to the Mineola train station to make the 4:54 to Penn.

Most afternoons, Dad was home by four p.m. When we came home from school, Mom would instruct me, Aidan, and whatever children she was looking after to take a seat at the kitchen table where we'd have a snack before getting on with our homework. When we lived in the house on Weybridge, Mom and I would walk to the end of the path leading up to our house, and wait. When Dad rounded the corner, I'd run to him and he'd carry me the rest of the way home. In the new house, I just chose the seat closest to the window so I was the first to see Dad coming up the driveway. He'd come in, say hi to us kids, kiss Mom on the cheek, and chug a glass of water before going out to the garage to work on the extension.

After clearing our books and setting the table for dinner, I'd take a seat on one of the high-top stools at the counter across from the sink. If Dad was carving a chicken breast or slicing roast beef, he'd reach under the sink and pull out a big orange plastic container. He'd pump three pumps worth of orange goo into his blackened hands, and begin lathering.

"All right, Smedley," he'd smile at me, "gimme that H_2O!"

I'd turn the faucet to the right and inhale the orange scent—not like the fruit, though. More like orange sherbet—like the *Flintstones* Push-Up pops you used to be able to get from the ice cream man. Dirt, dust, and grime seemed to disappear like magic. He'd turn the faucet to the left, shake off the water, and hold his palms up to show me his work. "All gone."

Once dinner was finished, he'd go back to the extension while Aidan and I cleared and wiped the table and swept the floor. Most nights, Dad would continue working until Aidan and I were just about to go to bed, or shortly after we'd fallen asleep. On Fridays, he wouldn't get home from the city until the TGIF lineup on TV was almost over; by the time we woke up on Saturday, he was either in the city or working on the extension . . . until May.

Dad loved planning vacations and took pride in the execution. Once he and Mom decided the dates, the countdown began. If we were going somewhere new, Dad would go to Barnes & Noble and buy the Frommer's a month or two beforehand, to get a feel for the area. A week before the trip, Dad would sit at the kitchen table after dinner with a map spread out, debating which route to take.

We always drove—even if we were going to Florida. We'd cruise to the sounds of Simon & Garfunkel, Van Morrison, and The Police with the windows down and Dad at the wheel. Sure, it was cost-effective, but I also think driving let Dad feel free.

Packing the car was where Dad found his true glory. There was nothing Dad loved more than fitting something into the car that Mom had declared as "never going to fit." He packed with Tetris-like accuracy, and took pride in the fact that we never had to purchase one of those containers that went on the roof. Everything always fit in the car.

"Say, 'Goodbye, house!'" Dad would announce as we pulled out of the driveway.

"Goodbye, house!"

"Say a prayer we get there safe," Mom would add, placing her hand on the angel attached to the passenger-side visor. Each of us received the same one when we got our cars—a silver angel holding a banner that said, *Angel of the Highway, protect us.*

Until I was ten, my family and I would spend the first two weeks of July at Lake George with the Roses and their two sons, Mikey and Jesse. Floyd Rose was Dad's best friend from work, and I loved that his wife's first name was Rose, transforming her into Rose Rose when they married.

We spent our days running barefoot around the black-top path that formed a makeshift cul-de-sac, bordered by cabins. The volleyball net had seen better days.

Dad and Floyd could be found by the lake, Heinekens in their hands, profanity in their mouths, work behind them.

On particularly hot summer days, when the stench of garbage couldn't be ignored and the sweat beneath my breasts began dripping and fusing with my shirt, I could hear the creak of the lawn chairs where Mom and Rose shared daiquiris and the secret to perfect chocolate chip cookies. We ate charcoal-topped burgers and hot dogs and caught fireflies when the sun went down.

Our last Fourth of July, we went into town and set up blankets in the park to watch the fireworks. I had to go to the bathroom, and Dad took me to the ice cream shop on Main Street. They said restrooms were for customers only, so we split a strawberry cone when I came out.

Outside, I took one lick and watched the pink scoop fall onto the sidewalk.

"Jesus Christ, what are you doing?" he shrieked.

"It fell," I whimpered.

"I see that. Don't you know how to eat ice cream?" he laughed.

He bought another cone, sat me on the bench outside, and asked if I had a good grip. I nodded.

"Okay, now listen, this is very important. Whenever you get a cone—especially when you get it from a girl—you gotta push the top down with your tongue. But. Be careful not to crack the cone. Come on, let me see you do it."

I placed my tongue flat against the top of the fresh scoop, pushed down, and watched the big scoop bulge outward.

"Now, take a long lick up the side before it gets melty

and starts dripping down your hand. That a girl! The key is to use as few napkins as possible. That's how you eat ice cream and save the planet."

That night, Mikey and I took our s'mores down to the dock and looked for the Big Dipper. He kissed me on the cheek and said he'd marry me if I wanted him to. Lung cancer killed his father by Christmas, and Dad decided not to go back to Lake George.

We started going to theme parks—Hershey, Busch Gardens, Universal Studios. Dad and Mom would wake at six, go for a walk, and then wake Aidan and me to get us ready for the day. Aidan and I would schlep sleepy-eyed into the elevator and groan when Dad dragged us toward the complimentary continental breakfast.

"It's included in the price of the room—you gotta eat!"

"But we're not hungry!"

"You gotta eat because we're not stopping somewhere in the park in an hour because you didn't feel like eating now," Dad would say as Mom slipped fruit into her backpack.

After breakfast, we'd pile into the Tahoe. The moans continued as Dad circled the parking lot for the perfect space, which always felt like miles from the entrance. After our family made it through the turnstiles and received stamps that never seemed to wash off our hands, Mom would begin applying the sunblock. She'd slather Aidan and me in white goo that wouldn't disappear no matter how much we rubbed.

We always arrived an hour before the park opened so Dad could grab a map and begin devising a plan of attack.

"Let's start at the back of the park and then work our way counterclockwise."

"Why?"

"Because people are lazy and always go to what's at the front of the park. No one is going to be in the back, and then we'll work our way back while everyone leaves and makes their way into the park. Now Rowan, you run ahead and get a place in line, and don't let anyone push you around."

"Okay," I'd beam.

Dad was my coaster buddy. We rode each coaster five times. The first time was usually wherever we could get a seat. Then we'd wait to ride in the very front row and the very last row, once in the daytime and once at night, because "there's nothing like a coaster at night."

No matter how many times we rode the same coaster, though, we were never ready for the flash capturing our picture, available for purchase at the ride's exit. If the picture was really funny, Dad would get his wallet from Mom and buy me a photo keychain.

Mom waited at the exit because her sensitive stomach couldn't handle the speed. I used to think Aidan waited with her to keep her company. It was only when he got older that we discovered he had a fear of heights. But Mom and I still had our tradition of riding the carousel and splitting a funnel cake afterward.

And then one summer, I didn't care how many days were left in the countdown. There was a boy I liked at home, and if I left for two weeks, some other girl could swoop in and get him to fall in love with her before I could. I stopped asking Dad about Eric Clapton and Pink Floyd, opting to put in my headphones at full volume. I didn't eat at the continental breakfast, and I bought over-priced pretzels with my babysitting money.

The Malaysians arrived on a Tuesday, and slept in Nana's apartment until Thursday morning.

When I walked up the driveway from school on Thursday afternoon, I saw who I assumed to be Gerard and James with Aidan shooting a basketball into a hoop that had previously hung unused over the garage. The girls were sitting on our deck—I couldn't tell who was braiding and who was sitting Indian-style. All I noticed was how their eyes disappeared when they smiled, just like mine.

It wasn't how the skin of their upper eyelids covered the inner angle of their eyes, which were dark brown, like mine. It wasn't the flatness of their faces or the darkness of their hair. It was the way I hadn't realized I was alone . . . until now.

"Hell-oh!" I don't know why I was speaking so loudly or slowly. "My. Name. Is. Row. An."

"Rowan," the girl on the floor sighed, rising to her feet. She opened her arms, pulled me in close, and said, "I'm Danielle."

On Friday night, the adults took us to Blockbuster before they went out for dinner. The boys rented *The Fast and the Furious*, the girls, *Legally Blonde*. We ate pizza in the basement—James took all the pepperonis off his slice but didn't want a plain one because he liked the flavor. None of them had ever tasted microwave popcorn or Sour Patch Kids and were instantly impressed by both.

While the boys watched their movie, the girls and I

headed up to my room. Two weeks prior to The Malay-sians' arrival, Dad finished painting over the pink walls with Caicos turquoise. Mom promised I could pick the color if I made the honor roll. That was months ago, and she'd finally made good. Sure, the walls no longer matched the pink carpet, but I liked it that way.

My bed—a twin with a French-style fleur-de-lis pat-tern atop the brass bed frame—was draped with the same floral print as my curtains, the hallway runner, and the living room couches, and was shoved into the corner to make room for the queen air mattress. I wasn't much for posters, but had a ton of CDs and a Case Logic binder to hold them. In the opposite corner sat the purple bubble chair Michelle had grown fond of, along with the dresser where I kept the stereo.

"You better hope you don't pop that chair," Danielle laughed as Michelle struggled to get comfortable.

Although Michelle, fourteen, was three years younger than I, and only a year younger than Danielle, she was several inches taller than us both. Danielle's old clothes clung to Michelle tightly, and the resentment was ap-parent. I wonder if she also resented how Danielle's full cheeks, her long black hair, and her ability to fit into my sequined halter tops led people to think it was we who were sisters.

"Shut up, Danielle!" Michelle snapped back. "I love this chair." The plastic squeaked against her body as she adjusted. "Seriously, it's the best."

"Pick a color, Danielle."

"There are so many—I can't choose!"

In the bathroom, directly opposite my bed, was my collection of nail polish. By this time, I probably had about fifty colors—I had even paid for some of them.

"So, pick ten and I'll do each of your fingers a different color."

"Okay," she laughed.

"What are you guys going to wear tomorrow to the family reunion thing?"

"I don't know," Michelle said between flips of *Cosmo Girl*. "But would you please please please straighten my hair?"

While Danielle had opted to grow her hair long, Michelle's came to just above her chin, her soft, auburn waves making her look like she was fresh from the beach.

"Of course I will, but you can't show up with no clothes on. I don't know about how they do things in Malaysia, but here you gotta at least wear something," I teased.

"I just don't like anything I brought with me."

"You know what we should do? We should go to the mall!"

It was a great idea. Michelle needed help finding a Walkman for a boy she liked in Kuala Lumpur. He was in Danielle's grade and had taken an interest in her when he found out she was coming to the US.

"What about you, Danielle? You like anyone back home?"

"A few, but I don't think they like me. What about you? Do you have a boyfriend, Rowan?"

"So, there's this guy . . . his name is Cole," I said.

"Oooh," Danielle cooed, "Co-ole."

"Shhh," I said, hitting her with a pillow. "My mom's going to be home any minute!"

"What's he like?"

"I don't really know. I mean, he's cool. He has green hair and goes to Nassau."

"What's Nassau?"

"It's the community college around here. Anyway, he's really smart and he drives and I want to ask him to prom, but I don't know."

"Why don't you ask him?"

"Well, we went to the Sadie Hawkins Dance last year." I paused, taking note of the confused looks on their faces. "It's, like, a dance where the girls are supposed to ask the guys instead of the guys asking the girls. Anyway, we went together last year but I only think Mom let me go with him because he's my cousin's best friend."

"One of the cousins we're meeting tomorrow?" Danielle asked.

"No, no. This one's on my mom's side."

"So why isn't he your boyfriend?"

"I don't know. We, like, made out a few times before the dance, but the past few times I've visited him at the mall he, like, doesn't talk to me as much."

"Maybe he has a girlfriend?"

"Shut up, Michelle!" Danielle said, tossing a pillow at her.

"I don't know. I think it's just because Chris is always around and Cole doesn't want him to know. But when I told my mom I was thinking about asking Cole, she made this huge deal about him being older and stuff and I'm like, 'Have you seen some of the boys my age?' Plus, he's not that old! He's only, like, three years older than me. That's, like, nothing."

"Totally," they agreed.

As I painted the top coat onto Danielle's nails, I

thought back to the Sadie Hawkins Dance, and how things had changed between me and Cole. Prom was my last chance to get things back to the way they were that night.

The next day, Mom said there was too much to be done for The Malaysians' welcome party, and there was no way Danielle, Michelle, and I were getting a ride to the mall. Instead, we walked to Bagel Express and finished our chocolate milk on the way home. Danielle and Michelle had never tried Nesquik or bacon or bagels, and were fascinated by how much cream cheese can fit on such a small amount of bread.

When we got back, Michelle put the *Moulin Rouge* soundtrack in my stereo.

"*Voulez-vous coucher avec moi, ce soir,*" we sang. "*Voulez-vous coucher avec moi . . .*"

By the time we finished the album, the entire contents of my closet were on the floor. We swapped clothes and crushes and stories until people began to arrive.

"Who is that again?" Danielle whispered.

"That's Aunt Audrey. She's married to Uncle Brad—Avery and Max are their kids. Avery is the same age as me."

"I don't think I'm ever going to remember all of them."

"Trust me, it took forever to get to know all of them—don't sweat it."

"Did you see where Michelle went?"

"Yeah, she's over there talking to Uncle Luke. I'm going to get some food—I'll save you guys a seat."

At the buffet, I was disappointed to see that despite

there being twenty kids under the age of eighteen, there were no chicken fingers or french fries to be found. I loaded up my plate with penne alla vodka and took a seat next to my cousin Avery at the kids' table.

"So Rowan," Avery began, "what's it like living with The Malaysians?"

"You mean Danielle and Michelle?"

"Yeah," she laughed, "how's it going?"

"It's good. Hey!" I waved Danielle and Michelle over to sit. "What did you get, the eggplant?"

"There was no pasta left!"

"Here, take some of mine and give me some of that. Save my seat—I'm going to the bathroom."

Avery was staring into a compact, Juicy Tube in hand, when I came out.

"So, what? You don't like us anymore?"

Avery's mother and my mother had this whole competitive thing going. Even though Avery was a year older, as a December baby she missed the cutoff, landing her in the same grade as me. She attended Mercy's rival, Sacred Heart Academy. She was slim, beautiful, and smart—assets my mother constantly reminded me about.

"What are you talking about?"

"Well, all of you seem to be in, like, your own little group."

"We're not in a group—they've just been staying with us, so they know us better."

"Just don't forget your real family—we're the ones who are going to be here when they leave."

"They *are* family, Avery."

"Yeah, but, like, not really. I mean, they're going to be gone soon and we're never going to see them again."

* * *

Danielle and I had a fight a week after the party. She dropped my hair straightener, cracking the ceramic plates, and I had to go to school with my hair in a bun. Mom insisted I didn't need a straightener—that my hair was naturally straight—but all the other girls straightened their hair, and I didn't want to be any more different than I already was. When I came home that afternoon, Danielle had bought me a Milky Way at CVS and I forgave her.

The following day, as I walked up the driveway from SAT prep, I saw their suitcases on the deck. I dropped my backpack on the curb and stormed into the house. Uncle Shane and Dad were having a beer at the kitchen table while Mom, Nana, and Jovinia chatted in the living room.

"Where's Danielle and Michelle?"

"They're in your room doing last-minute checks," Uncle Shane said nonchalantly, as if they always performed "last-minute checks" in my room.

"Rowan, why don't you go up and get changed and tell the girls to come down? We're all going to go out to dinner," said Dad.

"I don't want to go to dinner!" I screamed, running past him.

My bedroom door was open; Michelle was planted in my bubble chair and Danielle was kneeling beside the open suitcases on the floor. There was nothing to say.

That night, Danielle, Michelle, and I decided to sleep on the air mattress together. We linked arms in the hope that our parents would pause at the thought of separating us. Yet somehow, we wound up outside the house on Elderberry—a minivan taxi in the driveway. Michelle was first in the van—she couldn't deal and I hated her for it. Danielle and I held hands, and for the first time, I felt the heartbeat of another human being within me. We were bound by something greater than a shared last name and slanted eyes—we were family. The blood running through us wasn't the same, but we belonged to each other.

"Don't forget to e-mail me," she said, pulling me in close.

"I won't."

"You'll have to tell me how prom goes."

"Please don't go."

"Come, Danielle!" Shane said, handing the last of the suitcases to the driver.

"Dad!" I yelled. "Can Danielle stay?" I didn't know why the thought hadn't occurred to me sooner.

"Can I?" Danielle asked.

"You said they have dual citizenship, so why can't she just stay? She doesn't want to leave anyway."

"Rowan," Mom said sternly, "stop it. It's time to be a grown-up."

"No, she can—she can stay. She has every right! She can go to Mineola High School and next year I can leave Mercy and I can go there too!"

Danielle was pleading the same case to her parents. We didn't need an answer right now—we just needed to make them late enough to miss the flight.

"Danielle, say goodbye to Rowan and let's go. Now."

In the end, Dad pried us apart and the taxi door closed.

Danielle didn't come back.

* * *

Mom let me skip school the next morning, and the morning after that. The weekend came, and she continued to indulge my moping. By Monday morning, she'd had enough and dragged me to the end of the block by the collar of my sweater. I slumped into seat on the bus, while the edge of my collar hung close to my elbow.

The smell of hibiscus and rafflesia faded more quickly than the memory of life with Danielle and Michelle. We exchanged e-mails for a few weeks, but as June grew closer, I surrendered to prom fever, and lost myself in the decorations committee and theme possibilities.

CHAPTER SIX

NURSE FINISHES CHECKING OFF BOXES on the chart when the phone rings. She walks toward the phone hanging on the wall and I wonder how she's going to pick up the right line since almost all the lights are blinking. I hear the words "preliminary exam," "police report," "victim." She nods, says, "But . . ." nods, "but . . ."

It occurs to me that while there is most certainly a protocol, Nurse doesn't know it. Nurse doesn't encounter many victims. Nurse says on the phone she doesn't know if SANE is a two extension or a three extension. Nurse rolls her eyes and hangs up.

"I'm sorry, sweetie, but it looks like the front desk made an error. You're not supposed to be here."

"What?"

"You need to go to the SANE Center." Nurse sees I'm not getting it. "The SANE Center," she repeats, exasperated. "It's over on Community Drive about two miles from here—"

"But, like, what *is* that—the SANE Center?"

"The SANE Center is Long Island Jewish Hospital's Sexual Assault Nurse Examiner Program. They'll be able to provide you with the proper care," Nurse states, rummaging in the drawers by the sink before placing a photocopy of a map with faded print beneath it on the counter. "These are directions to the SANE Center. If you don't have a vehicle, you can go to the front desk and the admin can coordinate transportation for you. Do you have any questions?"

"What's going to happen there?"

"To be honest, I don't know, baby. I don't have that kind of training. All I know is that's where you gotta go to get right."

I wonder if this is the universe's way of telling me the lie has gone far enough—that I don't have what it takes to see it through. That I'm not really in need of medical attention. That there isn't anywhere I can go—that I will never be right.

Things had been weird between Cole and me ever since the Sadie Hawkins Dance. We'd stopped making out in the Journey's stock room, and our calls got shorter and shorter. Still, I was convinced if I could just get him to senior prom, everything would fall into place.

But Mom wouldn't hear it—he's too old, he doesn't respect the rules, he has green hair. We couldn't agree on my date, my shoes . . . my dress.

"I don't want to wear this dress!" I screamed, hurling the red Delia's gown into the hallway.

"Too bad, because it's the only one you're going to get."

"That's what you think. I have my own money."

"Oh yeah?" she laughed, coming to face me in the hallway, "What are you going to do? Walk to the mall?"

"I'd rather walk there than wear this," I said, stepping on the dress and twisting my feet.

I'd done it now. She took two steps forward and lowered her voice, "Pick that up. Now."

"No."

I was sick of her shit. Sick of being told what to wear and what time to be home. Sick of watching my friends hang out with whomever they wanted, whenever they wanted. Sick of being told the guy I loved wasn't up to her standards. Sick of *her*.

"I said pick it up now."

"I don't care. You're not my real mother, anyway."

It took her a minute, but eventually she brushed the tears away from her eyes, snatched the dress, and unzipped the back. She rolled up the gown and walked toward me. Instinctively, I ran to my room, closing the door behind me.

In her fury, she kicked the door open, the doorknob getting stuck in the wall. She backed me into a corner and threw the dress over my head.

Our arms got tangled, our hair messy, eyes puffy. Eventually, she pulled it downward, stepped back, and said, "That's a beautiful dress, Rowan. Whoever bought it for you must love you very much."

"I hate you!"

There are things I didn't know: I didn't know I'd say this to her again and again over the years. I didn't know I'd be spending my adult life trying to make it right. And I didn't know that eventually I'd have to come to terms with the fact that I can't. All I knew then was that she cried first, and I won.

Valentina and Laura were booking the limo, Sophia was

handling the corsages, and Madison's dad was letting us use his beach house in the Hamptons for after prom. My only responsibility was finding a date, and it wasn't going well.

"Journey's Roosevelt Field, James speaking—how can I help you?"

"Hey James, it's Rowan," I said, twirling the phone cord around my finger.

"What up, little mama? How's it hangin'? Haven't seen you here in a while."

"You know—SATs and crap."

"I remember those—bummer."

"Yeah, total bummer."

"You looking for your cuz?"

"Actually, I'm looking for Cole."

"Sure, he's right here—yo Cole! Phone!"

"This is Cole."

"Hey!"

"Oh, Rowan . . . hey."

"What's up?"

"Nothing," he answered curtly. "I'm at work."

"Oh," I mumbled to myself.

"Do you need something? Because I kind of have to go—"

"Cole," I heard a familiar voice say, "who you talking to?"

"Is that my cousin?" The voice was closer now. "Here, gimme that. Rowan, is that you?"

"Hey, Chris."

"Rowan, you can't call here, okay? This is my job—it's not cool."

"I was just—"

"Look, this little crush you have on Cole—it was cute, but it isn't funny anymore, okay?"

"I don't have a crush on him," I said defensively.

"Fine, you don't have a crush on him. But whatever it is, you gotta let it go. You have to stop calling here."

"Okay," I murmured.

"I've gotta get back to work. Next time you come to the mall, let me know and we'll hang out, all right?"

"Yeah, okay."

I stopped bringing up Cole's name at the dinner table, and made a point not to browse the south side of the mall on Friday nights with Valentina. Cole and I were over, but worse than that, Delia's was directly diagonal from Journey's—their selection of prom dresses clearly visible, leaving me no choice but to wear the red dress Mom had bought me.

As prom inched closer, so did graduation. Mom had become friendly with Mrs. Panarelli during Meet-the-Teacher Night, and had asked if there were any brilliant math students looking for some extra cash, as my trig average continued to plummet. Even though the SATs were behind me, I still had to pass math.

"I really don't want a tutor, Mom," I whined.

"You're going to need good scores to get into a good college," she said, placing some broccoli on my plate.

"Mom, I hate broccoli!"

"Is there anything you *do* like?"

"I like not being forced to spend an hour of my day studying dumb math I'm never going to use in my life."

"You think you're never going to use math?" Dad laughed. "I use math every day!"

"Writers don't need math, Dad."

"Writers don't add? Writers don't measure things? Writers don't use time?"

"Oh my god, you guys are so retarded."

"Rowan, don't say that," Mom said. "You're getting a tutor, you're going to get into a good school, and you're going to eat that broccoli."

Jamie was about a foot shorter than I, with thick black hair which never seemed to deviate from her bobbed haircut and glasses. One of the only other Asian girls at OLMA, Jamie seemed to think this made us kin.

Mom loved the fact that Jamie was also adopted from Korea. Jamie had pictures of herself as a baby in Hanbok. She knew her Korean name, spoke some Korean, ate kimchi, went to church on Sunday, and was bound for Susquehanna University on a partial scholarship.

In between teaching me about sine, cosine, and tangent, Jamie confessed she thought it strange I didn't want to know more about my Asian roots.

"Because I'm not Asian," I said.

"But you *are*," she argued.

"No, I'm really not." I wasn't denying my Asian-ness out of some loyalty to Mom and Dad. Sure, I was grateful. I knew Mom and Dad had done me a major solid and saved me from endless days in a rice paddy or a windowless warehouse assembling iPhones. It's just that "Asian" had never been a word I'd used to describe myself—it wasn't who I was.

"You aren't curious about where you come from? I mean, I know we're lucky to be adopted, but that doesn't mean you can't know more about where you come from."

I hated how people acted like being adopted was some kind of fucking miracle. Everyone wants to tell you how lucky and blessed and fucking fortunate you are. "You know," they say, "when you think about how many unwanted children there are in this world, it's nice to see two people like your parents giving one of those kids a loving home."

I found Asians to be the worst. I only really saw people who looked like me when I was getting a dress hemmed or needed a manicure, but it was always the same exchange.

"Where you from?" the conversation would begin.

"Mineola," I'd say.

"No," they'd chuckle. "You Chinese? Japanese?" Even to Asian people, China is the default for where all people with slanted eyes must be from. "Korean?"

I'd nod. It felt like a lie.

"*Annyeonghaseyo*," they'd say excitedly.

My manicurist, Mei, taught me the proper response is, "*Bangapsumnida.*"

"I don't speak Korean."

They'd be shocked. They'd always be shocked. "Why?"

"I'm adopted." They'd nod, although they wouldn't know what this meant. They weren't listening. "My parents are white."

"Why you no learn?"

I'd shrug. I didn't know. I'd have no acceptable answer.

They'd offer to teach me. They'd invite me to their churches and show me pictures of their single sons—as if their wanting me made the fact that BioMom didn't okay.

* * *

"You really don't want to know about Korea?" my tutor Jamie persisted.

"Nope," I replied, "not even a little bit."

"Well, if you ever change your mind and want to—"

"I'm good, thanks. If we could just do the triangles or whatever . . ." I trailed off. I think it's the only time in my life I've ever shown enthusiasm for mathematical education.

Waiting for Jamie's mother to pick her up felt longer that day. I don't know if it was because I didn't want to be Asian or because I told her triangles were stupid. Either way, I didn't care. I just wanted her gone.

"Who's that in the front seat?" I asked, as the Volvo pulled into my driveway.

"That's my brother."

"Oh, I have a brother too. Mom! Jamie's mom is here!"

Mom rushed outside to meet Mrs. Feretic. Normally, I'd have dumped Jamie and let her face the hour-long farewell between our moms alone in the car, but there was something about the boy in the front seat. I followed her outside.

Upon seeing Jamie and me emerge from the house, the boy in the front seat automatically unclicked his seat belt, opened the door, and got out to move into the backseat.

"Thanks, Trav," Jamie said, climbing into the front seat.

"No problem."

"Your name is Trav?" I asked with a smirk.

"Travis." He smiled, extending his hand.

"Rowan."

We talked about our mutual disdain for math while

Jamie randomly interjected facts about right triangles.

"SATs—man," he sighed, running his fingers through his hair, "I'll be taking those next year. But at least I'll have a big room to study in!" He nodded toward Jamie.

"You're not getting my room, Trav. Now get in the car."

"C'mon, Travis—we're leaving!" Jamie's mom called.

"See you later," he said, hopping into the car.

"See you."

Mom was impressed with the new initiative I was taking in mastering the Pythagorean theorem, and happily let me use the cordless to call Jamie for extra help. I couldn't help it if Travis happened to get the phone before Jamie could answer.

"So, I'm officially going to pass math."

"Really? Great!"

"Thanks. The thing is, I won't really be able to call as much because, like, you know."

"Oh, yeah, that's right. That sucks. I really like talking to you."

"I like talking to you too. Actually, I wanted to know if you wanted to, uh—I wanted to know if you wanted to go to this dance with me. You have to get, like, dressed up and stuff and it's totally cool if you don't—"

"You want me to go to prom with you?"

"I mean, yeah, but only if you really want to."

"Sure! I'd love to go!"

"Really?"

"Of course! When is it?"

Now, the entire prom had Mom's stamp of approval—my dress, my date, my friends. We danced and laughed and Travis even kissed me at night's end. When he called the next day, and the one after that, we talked for hours before Mom kicked me off the phone and told me it was time for dinner.

Travis seemed happy to know another person who was adopted, who understood what it meant to grow up in a neighborhood where no one looks like you, who wanted to know about where we came from. But I wasn't really that person. He spoke of his plans to apply for a passport on his eighteenth birthday—to travel to Korea and find his mother . . . his real mother.

"We could go together," he proposed.

"No," I said, "I don't want to do that."

He was shocked. "Why? Don't you want to know who she is? Why she gave you up?"

I did want to know. Oftentimes, it felt as though my heart were made of the questions surrounding BioMom, and that its beat was fueled by the need for answers. But I knew there was a possibility, however minute, that when I did find BioMom, there would be children alongside her. I knew there was a possibility BioMom just didn't want *me*. I stopped taking Travis's calls.

Mom went into all-out college-preparation panic in the weeks following prom. Despite having put a deposit down on the school of my choice, Mom left applications for Hofstra and Adelphi on my desk. I found her desperation to keep me on the island and under her control laughable.

My fights with her were constant and relentless. She was merciless in her quest to get me into a good, *local* college, unrelenting in her fear that I didn't have what it took to get there. There was no time for friends, for boys, for fun.

I didn't realize all she wanted was for me to have power over my own destiny, and thought a college education would give me the tools to harness and wield that power. I didn't know her only desire was for me to have the best of things, and that she didn't have the words to tell me.

After the fights came the silence, which seemed to last between Mom and me until the day I left for college. Dad would relay any requests I had to Mom, and she'd scream at him for indulging me, for taking my side, for passing along my messages. When my requests were denied, I'd lie about where I was going, who I was with, get caught and grounded, only to do it all over again.

Mom seemed hell-bent on keeping me away from boys. Now, I wonder if she knew it's because men wound women in impossibly cruel fashions. I wonder if she knew what I was searching for, and hoped keeping me in my room would allow me the time and space to find it.

Either way, I was glad to choose a school in Pennsylvania, and rolled my eyes when she hugged me goodbye two months shy of my eighteenth birthday.

CHAPTER SEVEN

GOOGLE MAPS TELLS ME I'VE ARRIVED as I drive past a cluster of brick buildings with no identifying qualities. I ask several people where I can find the SANE Center and am met with shrugs, confusion, fingers pointing nowhere.

"300 Community Drive?" I say to a man with a badge and a name tag.

"This is 300 Community Drive," he says, never looking away from the TV in his security booth.

"Is this the SANE Center?"

"I don't know about no SANE Center, but this is 300 Community. Parking is to the right, on the left."

"So, I go in here and make a right—"

"Make a right and then parking is on your left."

"Could you tell me—"

"Miss," he says, finally looking at me, "you're going to have to move along, there's cars behind you, please."

I decide not to thank him and roll up my window. There's no parking lot to the left of the right I've made, and every sign I encounter begins with NO. As I drive farther and farther away from what is allegedly 300 Community Drive, I scream obscenities.

A green Honda's taillights light up red, and I thank

god for this small mercy. When I pull in, I raise my middle finger to the sign beginning with *NO* directly in front of my Toyota.

I walk back to the security booth, determined to force the security guard to confess the location of the SANE Center.

By the end of my junior year of high school, I felt I had discovered the truth: Mom hated me. She hated me for not being her real daughter—for not looking and being exactly like her. That's why there were so many rules— they existed to make it easier for Mom to control my entire life and, by extension, control who I became. But no matter how hard she tried, no matter how many rules there were, I was never going to be who she wanted me to be. And so, I was determined to get out.

I applied to three schools: the College of Mount Saint Vincent in Bronxville, New York, University of Hartford in Connecticut, and Cabrini College in Radnor, Pennsylvania. All three were far enough away that I'd have to live in a dorm, close enough that an envelope of cash wasn't more than three days away, and all had either a creative writing major or minor.

Mom wanted me to apply to Hofstra, a twenty-minute bus ride from the house on Elderberry, or Adelphi.

"If you go to Adelphi, I can drop you off in the mornings," she observed over dinner one night.

"I don't want to go to Adelphi."

"What's wrong with Adelphi? It's one of the best schools on Long Island!"

"It's on Long Island—that's why. I hate it here!"

"Hey, hey," Dad interrupted, pointing his fork at me.

"I'll have you know Long Island has some of the most desired real estate in the country."

"Yeah, right," I laughed. "Who would want to live here?"

Mom left five checks on the pile of college applications on my desk. I took all five envelopes down to the mailbox, where Vinny picked me up each morning, but only mailed three. When I got to school, I tossed the Adelphi and Hofstra envelopes in the garbage can of the senior locker room.

Mom called the bank when the checks hadn't cleared eight weeks later. When they couldn't explain the anomaly, she called the schools, who informed her they'd never received an application for Rowan J. Kelly.

The fight Mom and I had that night was epic. It was the one time I thought she might actually hit me. I thought she was mad I'd gotten the best of her—that I'd taken charge of my own future. I didn't know all she wanted was for me to have the options and choices she never did.

In the following weeks, as our mailbox continued to go without news, part of me started to think Mom may have been right. Perhaps applying to only three schools to make a point had been a bit foolish.

If I didn't get in anywhere, I was headed for Nassau Community College, commonly referred to as the thirteenth grade among Long Islanders. I'd have to live at home, find a job, and get a car, unless I wanted to take the bus. Mom would still have power over me—my comings and goings, my friends . . . I'd never get a boyfriend.

* * *

During junior high, after I'd completed the Catholic High School Entrance Examination, the scores were sent to the three high schools I'd listed, but I was still required to submit a formal application to each school individually.

The mail arrived before I did. When I came home from school, there was an envelope set out for me on the kitchen table. It had been opened and taped back together. I sat on the bench, and saw the seal of Mercy in the corner.

Mom and Dad ran in from the kitchen to watch me discover what they'd already found out: I'd gotten in. They hugged and kissed and congratulated me. They told me how Nana would be thrilled to know her granddaughter would be continuing the legacy of Kellys at Our Lady of Mercy Academy.

It was the first time I'd ever felt like I'd done something right—that I'd made Mom proud. That for once I wasn't the letdown I'd always been. So, I signed my name on the acceptance form, and let Mom write a check for the deposit.

The acceptance letter from Holy Trinity came the following week. Mom said it wouldn't be a big deal if I wanted to change my mind, that the deposit wasn't an issue . . . that it was my choice. I chose not to disappoint her and resented this for the next four years.

The College of Mount Saint Vincent was the first to accept me, followed by the University of Hartford. Mom left their letters unopened on the third step of the stairs, along with my *Rolling Stone* magazine. Despite barely sharing any details of my life with her, she knew which school I was waiting on.

The letter from Cabrini College came on a Friday. It was still cold outside, so I'd worn tights instead of knee-highs. They were a pain to get on, and I hated how they needed to be washed every night to retain stretchiness for the next day.

I dropped my backpack on the laundry room tile, figuring I'd come back for it later, since homework could be done anytime. Mom and Dad were sitting at the kitchen table—a bright white #10 envelope between them.

Their faces lit up as I walked in and Mom excitedly pointed to Cabrini's custom return address, when Emma ran in.

At eleven, her loose curls hung just above her tailbone, a few strands tucked behind each of her diamond-studded ears. She was tall for her age, almost reaching my shoulder. The years had given Emma's green eyes a touch of brown—it was no wonder she seemed to be the center of attention.

"Marie," Emma said to my mom, "can you put a movie on?"

"Give me a few minutes," Mom said, to my surprise. She always had time for Emma. "I'm busy just now, but I'll be in in a little while, okay?"

"Okay," Emma sighed, going back to the den.

"You didn't open it this time," I said, picking up the envelope.

"It's not mine to open."

"What about Mercy's?" I asked.

"That was different," Mom said. "I didn't want your first acceptance . . . if it had been bad news I wanted to—I just, I just didn't want—" She took a deep breath. "I just want you to be happy, okay?"

I nodded and went to tear the envelope open before she stopped me.

"Whatever it is, Rowan, it's okay. If you don't get in, you can always go to Mount Saint Vincent or Hartford and transfer to Cabrini if you still want to go there. It's not the end of the world—it'll be okay. If being a writer is what you want to do and Cabrini is where you want to go to do it, we'll find a way."

I nodded, tore open the envelope, and said, "I got in."

She and Dad screamed, throwing their arms around me.

"Aidan," Dad called up the stairs, "get down here!"

"Why?"

"To tell your sister congratulations—she's going to college!"

It wasn't until I left Long Island that I discovered not all diners were open 24/7 and sandwiches did not typically come with almost a pound of meat crammed between two slices of bread. I also learned no one seemed to know what or where Long Island was. I found this to be unsurprising. After all, Long Island had proven to be the apex of where absolutely nothing happened.

People were shocked to learn Long Island was part of New York, and not a separate entity. I began describing it as the tumor hanging off the state. Real Manhattanites laugh at this—happy there's at least one Long Island native who knows they're not a *real* New Yorker.

"Are you close to New York City?" the non–New Yorkers ask.

"Yeah, I guess. The city is, like, not even an hour away."

They want to know if I go there all the time, if I've

ever seen anyone get shot . . . if I've gone to see *Saturday Night Live*.

I don't have the stomach to tell them that despite living forty minutes from the City That Never Sleeps, I never go there. That my friends and I prefer to drive across the same few highways, which all seem to go to the same place, with the windows down and the music up. That no matter where we go, what we do, or how many strip malls we pass, we always wind up at the same diner, ordering from the same laminated menus, as we lament living in the most boring place, with the most boring people, with nothing to do.

So when asked if I've seen anyone get shot, I say, "Yes. Yes, I've killed a man."

With less than a week left until we drove down to Pennsylvania, Mom and I still hadn't made up. I could take my pick of reasons: I'd chosen to go to the mall with Valentina to shop for college clothes instead of with her; I told her I didn't want a stupid family dinner at home because I was more concerned with making an appearance at Valentina's parents' barbecue; and I wasn't being much help when it came to packing—I never did organize my clothes up to her standards anyway.

The real reason Mom was angry was because I thought I didn't need her. I was college bound, which meant her days of telling me what to do and who to be were over.

"Say, 'Goodbye, house!'" Dad commanded as we pulled out of the driveway.

Aidan and I mumbled a half-hearted farewell to the house on Elderberry as Mom instructed us to say a prayer for our safe arrival. I slipped my headphones on while Aidan turned to his Nintendo DS.

At the last minute, I turned toward the back of the Tahoe to catch one last glimpse of the house on Elderberry through the cardboard boxes and containers full of clothes taking up the trunk. It was hard to believe the entirety of my existence could be packed into the back of a car.

Cabrini College sat on 112 acres of Pennsylvania bumblefuck, half an hour outside Philly, and appeared to be in a constant state of autumnal transformation. Even on the scalding August day of freshman check-in, the trees looked as if their leaves had caught fire—shimmering auburn, orange, and gold against the sunlight.

The incoming class of 2008 was no greater than 350 boys and girls looking to stave off adulthood, and I was no different. At seventeen, all I wanted was enough miles to prevent Mom and me from sharing a roof, and now here I was.

I got out of the Tahoe with a smile on my face and sprinted to the registration table at the front of Founder's Hall, scanning the check-in sheet to see if Erin had arrived.

At 5'10", Erin had a good six inches on me. She had dirty-blond hair, broad shoulders, and ears like Dopey. We'd met during Cabrini Day of Service, on the second day of Accepted Students Weekend, and I loved her instantly.

Founded by the Missionary Sisters of the Sacred Heart of Jesus in 1957, Cabrini College was not only committed to educating the future of America, but also to providing its students with a sense of responsibility to their community. Erin and I were assigned to the Habitat for Humanity group to help gut one of the row homes in North Philly.

Erin was spackling the front of the house, while I was put on top of a ladder and told to use a sledgehammer to take out the ceiling. After observing my lack of upper-body strength, Erin offered to switch, and I agreed happily.

"Just so you know," she said, holding the ladder as I climbed down, "I'm not a lesbian."

"Okay," I laughed.

"Seriously, I'm not. Everyone thinks I am because I'm on the basketball team, but I'm really not. I like guys."

"Me too."

I held the base of the ladder as she climbed up and handed her the sledgehammer. Erin took one swing at the ceiling and the light fixture came down on the two of us. We were excused for the rest of the day, and she still has a small scar on her nose.

Once we returned to campus, we signed a roommate assignment form, exchanged numbers, and said we'd see each other soon.

"Erin's not here yet!" I called back to Dad.

Dad was the first to reach the registration table, then Mom, who hadn't spoken a word to me the entire trip down, and Aidan close behind. Dad made sure everything was okay with the deposit and signed all the forms since it would still be two months before I turned eighteen.

"It looks like you're in, uh," Dad began, scanning the documentation, "Woodcrest 303."

"Ugh," I groaned. "Erin and I wanted to get into Xavier."

"What's wrong with Woodcrest?" he asked, as we walked back to the car.

I didn't want to tell him I didn't spend four years in an all-girls Catholic high school to end up in the female-only building my freshman year of college. I went with, "I heard the rooms are smaller there."

"Well," Mom said, breaking her silence, "I hope you get used to sharing because no room is going to be as big as the one you have at home."

"You're talking to me now?" I said to her.

Nothing.

Mom remained silent as she helped Dad, Aidan, and me haul my life to the third floor, down the hall, and into a 192-square-foot room with no air conditioner. She brightened up when Erin's parents arrived, putting on a happy face and making small talk, but returned to the silent treatment once we got in the car and began searching for a restaurant to have our last meal as a family until Thanksgiving.

We ate in silence and returned to campus in silence. Dad got a little teary-eyed when he hugged me for the last time and I was sure the only reason Aidan actually said goodbye was because his DS had died.

"Take care of yourself, Smedley," Dad said. "Try not to cause too much trouble."

Mom put her anger aside long enough to give me a hug. She told me not to forget to check in at least four times a week and reminded me to send a copy of my class schedule.

"I will."

"Come here," she said, pulling me in for one more hug before taking a package out of her bag and handing it to me.

I unwrapped the paper to reveal a teal leather diary, with a belt buckled around it. The belt buckle was attached to a button underneath to keep the diary closed.

"It's to write all your adventures in," she said.

More than anything, I wanted to tell her I loved her, that I was sorry for the past few weeks, that I was going to miss her. "Thanks," I said.

"Now, don't forget to call—"

"I know, I know."

"Okay. I love you," she said, squeezing me one last time.

"Me too."

I called Mom once over the weekend before school started to tell her I'd mailed her the schedule and to let her know classes started Monday. Somehow, it was easier to talk to her with 130 miles between us. Mom seemed to really listen, like she wanted to know everything. When we hung up, I was surprised to see we'd been on the phone almost an hour.

That Monday, I picked up the phone to hear incoherent shrieking and thought she was calling to yell about the state I'd left my room in.

"I—I—"

"Mom? Is everything okay?"

"I've made you chocolate chip cookies every first day of school for—for—" she sobbed, "for thirteen years. And now, now you're off at college, and it's your first day of school, and I have cookies in the oven but you're not going to be home to eat them."

"Mom, it's okay," I said, trying to pack up for class.

"No, no, it's not. I just—you're my—my little pumpkin pie—"

"Look, Mom, I can't really talk right now. I gotta get to class."

"Okay, okay," she said, breathing deeply, trying to compose herself. "I love you."

"Love you too. Bye!" I said, closing my phone.

"Dude, come on," Erin said, "we're gonna be late."

Erin and I were walking to class the first time I saw Hunter. He was wearing a three-piece suit and smoking a cigarette outside Founder's Hall, the pinstripes of his vest and trousers perfectly aligned. He had on a black cowboy hat.

Hunter was tall and fit. The arms of his purple Oxford were tight against his muscles—the top button was undone and revealed a white T-shirt and chest hair beneath. He dressed with purpose and I longed to know what it was—for he seemed to be a man, and I knew nothing of men.

I didn't realize I was staring at him until I saw Erin was already at the top of the steps.

"What are you waiting for—an invitation?" she laughed.

As much as I didn't want to be late for my first class, I wanted to take him in—wanted to memorize his pale skin and green eyes. Wanted to burn the image of how his warm brown hair fit perfectly behind his pierced ear, and caught the light in all the right places, stopping at the nape of his neck.

He opened the door as we approached, and I noticed an unfinished tie dangling around his neck.

"Hi," I said, as we passed through the doorway.

He simply tipped his cowboy hat forward and said nothing.

Erin spanked her ass and galloped into the atrium of Founder's. I followed suit and attempted to lasso her— our laughter gathering the attention of those around us. We rode our invisible horses up the stairs and down the hall, coming to a halt outside Intro to Mass Comm.

Erin and I spent the first weeks of our freshman year sneaking boys into the dorm past visiting hours and going for joyrides in her Subaru, stealing random signs from the liquor stores on Upper Gulph Road. Our room was adorned with Mike's Hard Lemonade cutouts and Bud Light banners.

Eventually, our joyrides grew longer and we found ourselves cruising the empty Pennsylvania streets, the car vibrating to the rhythm of the best of the nineties, barely audible against our perfect recollection of the lyrics that had defined our youth.

On Halloween, Erin and I were outside Woodcrest waiting for Sporty, Ginger, and Posh Spice when Hunter walked by, dressed as a pirate.

"Hey," he said, walking toward us.

"Hey," we replied in unison.

"What's up?" I asked, in disbelief that I'd mustered the courage to speak.

"Nothing much. What are you doing tonight?"

"House 6's Halloween Hoedown," Erin said. "You?"

"Same. Uh," he mumbled, "are you going to the Hoedown too?" he asked, turning to me.

"Yeah. Yeah, I'm going."

He didn't know my name but asked if he could escort me to House 6. I looked to Erin, who gave me a smile before turning to Hunter. "Yeah, sure."

I was grateful for Hunter's arm since I hadn't learned how to walk in heels.

"So, do you have a name?"

"Rowan," I said. "My name is Rowan. What's yours?"

"I'm Hunter," he said, shaking my hand.

When we arrived at House 6 a few minutes later, he placed a cigarette between his teeth, motioning for me to come closer. "I need your hands."

I cupped my palms around his lips as he lit a match. Erin and the rest of the Spice Girls headed toward us. "Hey, I'm going to go in. See you in there?" I said to Hunter.

"I've got some business to take care of later so I might cut out early."

"Oh yeah?" I smiled. "What kind of business?"

"Just need to deliver something to a client of mine."

Aware of what he was saying, I looked from side to side before lowering my voice, "What? What are you delivering?"

"Goodies."

"Like drugs?"

"Hey," he hissed, pulling me close to him, "keep your voice down."

The only time I'd done drugs was on the hood of Cole's car at Jones Beach. I didn't know what Hunter was into—weed, cocaine, pills. But something about the way he held me close—how I could feel my heart beating faster against his chest in the October cold—made not knowing okay.

"Who's going to walk me home then?" I flirted.

"Here," he said, handing over his phone, "put your number in and I'll call you later."

"All right," I said, entering my digits, "it's in there. Now you're going to have to call me."

"If I call," he smiled, "you better answer."

Public Safety broke up the party after my second beer. I spotted Erin about to go upstairs with the Fresh Prince of Bel-Air and managed to grab her before the door shut. It took an hour and a half to get her back to Woodcrest and into bed. About to unhook my bra, I groaned when the phone rang, but answered in case it was Hunter. He asked me to meet him outside, and I said okay.

"Want to go for a walk?" he asked.

"Kind of cold, don't you think?"

"I'll lend you my coat."

We walked past the Dixon Athletic Center on the other side of campus. Across the field, he gave me a boost over the fence into the St. Davis Golf Club. On the other side, we lay by the eighteenth hole, watching our breath disappear into the October sky.

"Won't we get into trouble?"

"No, I come here all the time."

"How did you find this place?"

"Me and my dad used to play holes here."

"You don't anymore?"

"Not so much. Are you close with your parents?"

"I'm close with my dad," I said. "My mom—not so much."

"Why not?"

"My ass is wet," I laughed. I didn't want to talk about

Mom, so we talked about other things until my teeth began to chatter.

He gave me another boost and when we were both over, he took a step forward, forcing my back against the chain-link fence.

"Can I kiss you?" he asked.

I said yes.

"Wait, the pirate from Halloween? You didn't tell him it was your birthday?" Erin asked, throwing yet another top onto the "No" pile growing on our floor. I'd been eighteen for two weeks and we were finally going out to celebrate.

"It's not that I didn't tell him. I said it once and then never mentioned it again. We've only been doing whatever we're doing for, like, three weeks. I didn't want him to feel like I was saying it just so he'd get me something. Because then he'd feel like he *had* to get me something. Or worse, I didn't want him to forget and not get me anything. Or, worse than that, I didn't want to have to act surprised when he gives me the worst gift imaginable."

"Dude, you worry too much. Does this make my shoulders look big?"

"Not if you wear your hair down it won't."

She took out her ponytail and started combing. "So where does he think we're going tonight?"

"He knows we're going to Philly, he just doesn't know why. Speaking of which, I'm going to run over to New Res and say bye."

"What? The cab's going to be here in an hour!"

"I know, but I'm not going to see him all weekend. I'll be right back—promise! Don't leave without me."

* * *

"You look nice," Hunter said, opening the door.

"Well thank you," I said, doing a quick twirl. "I can't stay long—I'm meeting Erin and the girls soon."

"All right, take a seat. I'll be right back." Hunter disappeared into the kitchen. The second-year dorms were so much nicer than ours—complete with single rooms, kitchens, and their own showers.

The room went dark and a light began to flicker behind me. The aluminum foil pan looked as if it was about to buckle from the generous helping of frosting. A mountain of pink sprinkles populated the center of the cake and looked as if they had been fanned outward after being dropped by accident.

"You made me a cake?"

"Yeah, well, you were at the game your birthday weekend and had midterms and shit this week. I haven't really seen you, so happy birthday," he said, kissing me on the cheek.

"I didn't think you'd remember."

"Of course I remembered. You're my girl."

"Oh yeah?"

"Yes," he said, placing a kiss on my cheek. "You're always going to be mine. So, let's cut this thing and get into bed."

"I can't," I said between kisses. "Erin and the girls are waiting."

"But it's cold out there."

"I know."

"And it's warm in here."

"But—"

"And I have cake."

"I really can't," I said, getting up from the table. "Erin has been planning this and she'll be really mad if I don't go. Please don't be mad."

"I'm not mad. I just want to make sure my girlfriend knows how special she is to me."

"So, I'm your girlfriend now?"

"Yes. You are." He smiled, turning my phone off. "Now, hurry up and make a wish."

I closed my eyes and wished that Erin wouldn't get mad when I called and asked for a rain check.

Our first fight was over a shower. I was getting ready to leave his dorm and told him I'd be stopping by my room after class.

"Why?"

"I haven't seen Erin all week and I want to take a shower."

"There's a perfectly good shower here," he said.

"But all my girl stuff isn't here—"

"So what? All you need is soap and shampoo, right? Well, I have soap and shampoo."

"Well, I'd like to see Erin too. I feel bad about leaving her by herself in Mass Comm the other day. I forgot to tell her I was skipping."

"Who is he?"

"Who is who?"

"The guy you're fucking."

His tone was so matter-of-fact, I had to stop packing and look at him. Even angry, he was beautiful—the blond highlights hidden intermittently throughout his predominantly brown hair were natural. He'd taken my suggestion, and let it grow out so that a few strands often fell over his right eye. Still, there was something about seeing him in the middle of the doorway that worried me.

His arms were crossed over his chest, his stance wide. He was ready for an argument, and solid in his belief that somehow I could love another man.

"What are you talking about?" I laughed.

"Don't fucking play with me, Rowan."

"Are you insane? I'm not seeing some other guy."

"Yeah, well, then why can't you use the perfectly good shower here? That makes no sense."

"Seriously? I'm just going to take a shower and see my friend. Maybe if you let me keep some of my stuff here I wouldn't have to go across campus to take a fucking shower."

Hunter's hand hit me with such force that the inside of my cheek split against my teeth and sent blood against the white cinder-block wall. My cheek burned—the blood within prickling the skin where it had been struck. He looked as stunned as I was.

Dad always said love was built on trust. Trust that the other person would be honest about the things that matter, and the things that don't. Trust that they'd love you despite your flaws. Trust that they'd protect you from harm. Trust that they'd never hurt you on purpose.

Getting hit in the face violated that trust. I was hurt because I wasn't expecting it. I was hurt because Hunter was not who I thought he was.

"Fuck you."

I slammed the door behind me, ignoring him as he called out my name. Once in the stairwell, I pushed my way past those brave enough to take morning classes, hoping they couldn't see my shame. Outside, the concrete chilled my bare feet. I wasn't going back.

An hour later, there was a furious pounding on my dorm room door.

"Rowan! Come on, I know you're in there."

"Fuck off."

"Would you just talk to me?"

I didn't know then that I'd already forgiven him—that I'd continue to forgive him.

"There's nothing to talk about."

"I'm sorry. You know I would never hurt you."

"Obviously not," I said, flinging the door open.

"Look, I don't know what happened. I'm sorry, it's just—"

"What?"

"It's just that I don't want you to be with anyone else, okay? I—I fucking love you and I'm scared you're going to leave me."

"I love you too."

"You say that, but I've been hurt before and—"

"Look, I'm not Julie, okay? You want to go through my phone? Here," I said, chucking it at him. All I wanted was to prove what we had was ours—that I was going to protect it.

"I'm not going to go through your phone. Just . . . come here."

I opened my arms to him, and let him cry on my shoulder. I was captivated by the intensity of his passion—that the preservation of our love had driven him to violence. There was something seductive about how dangerous my potential departure made him. What we had was so grand that we were fighting one another. Maybe we had to destroy each other and piece ourselves together to form something that was both of us. He loved me, though, and that was enough for now.

CHAPTER EIGHT

"Hey Mack, it's Ernie down at 300, how you doin'? ... I'm good, good—kids are good too, thanks for asking. Listen, I got a girl here lookin' for the SANE Center. You know where that's at?"

I wait patiently as Ernie's eyebrows rise and his mouth opens wide. "Oh, no doubt, no doubt. I gotcha. I didn't real—yeah, yeah. I'll make sure she gets over there."

Ernie places the receiver onto the phone carefully, worried that any sudden movement will send me into hysteria. I assume Mack has told him what the SANE Center is, and what kind of women go there.

"So, miss, what you're going to do is go straight through those doors under where it says *Greene Emergency Center*. Once you're inside, just go to the desk and they'll get you where you need to go."

I say nothing and walk past him toward the Greene Emergency Center, where I would have logically ended up had his security booth not existed. When I enter, all I can focus on is the wall of pamphlets.

To my right, there is an acrylic brochure holder that goes from floor to ceiling. It is so massive that I walk toward it before making my way to the desk. My eyes scan the cartoon illustrations of people and unlabeled bottles of alcohol—*What Is Consent: Preventing Sexual Assault*; *Alcohol, Drugs & Sexual Assault*; *What to Do If Someone You Know Is Raped*.

As I walk I continue to scan the wall and the brochures begin to change. One has a name tag that reads, *Hello, I'm Being Abused: Domestic Violence—It's Never that Obvious*. Another has a stock image of hands clutching cell phones; the tagline reads, *The Power Is in Your Hands*.

Two years after meeting Hunter, I found myself outside the Radnor train station, approximately one mile from campus, at one in the morning.

I untucked my hair from behind my ears, and crossed my arms against my bare chest. The world could blame my nakedness on a lack of class or culture—no one had to know Hunter dragged me out of the house and down the stairs with no shirt and no shoes only an hour before.

The rain had gotten into my bones, filling me with a chill I knew I wouldn't be able to shake unless the sun came out in a few hours. As I approached the station, I considered my options: I could walk onto the platform and brave the people who board trains at one a.m., or I could hide out in the underpass and brave the people who walk through tunnels at one a.m.

I took a step toward the underpass. Voices made me stop, and I ran onto the platform, making eye contact with the only other person there—a black man with low jeans, talking on his cell phone. He wore a white wifebeater, and a black do-rag. There was a koi fish on his arm, and a silver chain hanging from his neck. His Timbs were the same Hunter once used to crack one of my ribs—the same Dad laced up before he went to work.

"Yo, hold up," he said into the phone, looking my way, "I'ma have to call you back."

He closed the same yellow Nextel Dad wore on his belt, and put his hands in the air. "Hey miss! Hey miss, can I help you?"

I stepped back while he adjusted his jeans and removed his shirt.

"Here," he said, tossing it to me, "that's for you. Put that on."

I hurriedly put the T-shirt on as he placed the phone on the ground and kicked it over to me. "Whoever you need to call—talk as long as you like. I'ma be right here."

I took the phone and flipped it open—2:14 a.m. The person I wanted to call had gone to bed hours ago. Our last words had been angry ones, and were exchanged almost two Thanksgivings ago. I promised the silence between us would last forever, as would the hate.

Deep breath. Dial. Ring. "Hello?"

Another deep breath. "Mom?"

Returning to Cabrini after winter break my freshman year was infinitely more awesome than my initial arrival months before. I seemed to have it all figured out—I finally learned the difference between a cappuccino and a latte, made friends with the cafeteria staff who would conveniently forget to charge me for fries, and memorized the locations of every free printer on campus. I was ready to kick the rest of my freshman year's ass.

When I went to check my first semester's grades, I got an error message stating I needed to make an appointment at the Office of Financial Aid. I called the office, and found myself sitting across from a slim blonde with glasses a few hours later.

"Miss Kelly, the way merit-based scholarships work is that you must obtain the merit upon which they are based and distributed. And it appears that you have not been attending class in quite some time."

"I can explain that. I was actually sick for, like, a week before Thanksgiving and I have a note here saying—"

"I am so sorry, Miss Kelly. But at this point, withdrawing is the only way to preserve your GPA."

"Like a leave of absence?"

"Unfortunately, you must be in good academic standing to take a leave of absence . . ."

"I'm sorry—I don't get this. Can't I just do some extra work or something? You can't just kick me out . . ."

"No one is kicking you out, Miss Kelly. I'm simply trying to explain your options. Your scholarship depends on your academic performance and, given your track record, we cannot renew your scholarship this semester. The registrar has withdrawn you from the classes you've registered for until full payment for the semester is received. Perhaps you can speak to your parents about taking out a loan."

I left the office frantic, staring at each person I passed as if they had the answer. If I didn't come up with $16,000 before the first day of classes, I was going to be sent back to the house on Elderberry. I wasn't thinking about how disappointed Mom and Dad would be, how embarrassing it was going to be telling friends and family I'd flunked out—all I cared about was being able to see Hunter.

I kicked the doors of Woodcrest open, stomped up the

six flights of stairs to my room, and slammed the door behind me, startling Erin.

"Dude," she said, taking note of my frenzied look, "are you okay?"

"Cabrini is kicking me out. Some bullshit about missing too many classes. They told me to make my parents take out a loan . . ."

"Dude, are you serious right now?" Erin asked.

"Yes, I'm fucking serious! Do you think I'd be here freaking out if I wasn't?"

"Honestly, I'm surprised you're here at all."

"What's that supposed to mean?"

"Rowan, I haven't seen you in, like, three weeks. I don't think you've slept here since Thanksgiving."

"What are you talking about? I just saw you at the Cavs game."

"Dude, we haven't had a home game in a month. You said you were going to come to the Villanova game but you fucking bailed . . . as usual."

"I told you I wasn't feeling well. Jesus, so I missed one game."

"Bullshit, Rowan. You were with *him*!"

"If you're talking about Hunter—"

"Of course I'm talking about Hunter. That's all we ever talk about anymore. Everything is about Hunter. Well, you know what? I hate Hunter!"

"You don't even know him!"

"You're right—I don't know him. How can I when he keeps you locked away in his room 24/7? I haven't seen you in weeks and you show up here—"

"I came here because you're my best friend!"

"How can you say that when you don't even talk to

me anymore? I've been worried about you. You never pick up your phone, you're never online. It's like he owns you!"

"You're way off."

"Look, I asked around and everyone says Hunter is a psycho. His last girlfriend broke up with him because he punched her for talking to another guy and he said he would kill her."

"Well, if my boyfriend slept with everyone on campus and then some, I'd probably want to punch someone too."

"I miss you, is all. I'm worried about you."

Erin's hair had been in a bun since I'd met her at orientation, a smile permanently affixed to her face. She was tall, broad, and married to the idea that it was acceptable to wear socks with her Adidas Adissage Slides. It was only now—with her eyes glassy and her voice uneasy— that I realized we'd never fought, we'd never disagreed. All we'd ever done together was laugh, until now.

"God, what are you—my mother? You don't need to worry about me. Hunter isn't crazy and his ex is a lying slut. You know, just because you can't get a boyfriend doesn't mean I have to spend every waking moment with you."

"So it's like that?"

"Yeah, it's like that."

Mom and Dad collected me two weeks later. I told Hunter not to come say goodbye—the last thing I needed was Mom laying into him.

"Well, I hope you're proud of yourself, Rowan," she said, closing the car door.

"You know what, Rowan?" Dad said. "Living away from home is tough. It's not for everyone. Maybe you can look into taking some classes at Nassau over the summer."

"Haven't you heard, Joseph? Our daughter doesn't go to class. I hope you understand what you've done here, Rowan—I really do."

"Shut up," I groaned.

"What did you just say to me?"

"Shut up. Just shut the fuck up!"

"Hey! Watch it, Rowan!" Dad said, reaching back to smack my knee. "Don't talk to your mother like that."

For the first couple of weeks, I didn't do much—watched some TV, ate macaroni and cheese, talked to Hunter every night. The distance was taking its toll on us both. Mom wouldn't let me have my cell phone at the dinner table, so if I missed his call, there'd be an angry voice mail waiting for me, demanding to know where I was and who I was with.

Toward the end of what would have been my first year in college, Hunter found out he'd scored a single room in House 6. With no check-in desk, it would make visiting much easier since I wouldn't have to be signed in, signed out, and then sneaked through the window so I could spend the night.

"Next year when I'm a senior, we're going to move off campus and get our own apartment."

"I can't wait," I sighed, taking off my black blazer and tossing it into the hamper. "I'm saving everything I can."

I'd gotten a job at the Jericho Terrace, a catering hall within walking distance of the house on Elderberry, to get Mom off my back. I thought it would shut her up, but now she was pushing for me to take classes at Nassau since summer was getting close.

"I'm sick of this every-other-weekend bullshit. Can't you work more hours?"

"Me too, but my parents don't want me to see you. Well, my mom doesn't want me to see you—she thinks this whole thing is your fault. She thinks I'm going to hang out with Erin. She knows I miss her, but if I go down there every weekend, she's going to get suspicious."

"Who cares? Once you have enough to come down here, I promise you'll never have to see her again. I won't let them take you away. Don't you want to be with me?"

"More than anything," I said.

"How much do you have already?"

"About $1,500."

"That's more than enough! I'm so proud of you, baby. Here's what you do."

I packed my blue Kipling bag with my passport, the money, my laptop, and a few of my favorite clothes. At two a.m., I opened the door of my bedroom slowly, stopping each time it creaked. Even though the carpet made getting down the hallway undetected easy, and even though she was asleep, I heard Mom moan, "Who's there?"

I froze, held my breath, and listened for the squeak of her and Dad's ancient bed frame as she turned over, before moving onto the real challenge: the stairs.

The first five steps, where the staircase wound and

curved around to the second floor, were no trouble. The main staircase was the problem. I stayed to the left, clinging to the bannister, for the first six steps, then switched to the right side, my back to the wall, for the remaining five, and jumped over the last one.

Mom washed the vinyl floors of our kitchen with Mop & Glo every Friday night, making them extra slippery. My socks acted like ice skates as I glided across the floor without a sound. At the back door, I singled out the house key and held the other keys in my fist to ensure a minimal amount of noise.

If I'd known what was to come, I'd have taken the time to memorize the house. To take in its smell, its shape, its essence, so its memory could comfort me when I felt most unsafe. If I'd truly known the man I was running to, I'd have woken Mom. I'd have fallen to my knees and begged for her help, her forgiveness, her love. If I'd known no amount of therapy would stop the nightmares, I'd have turned around and gone back to bed. But I didn't.

Outside, I continued to tiptoe since my parents always slept with the windows open. Once I passed the house on Elderberry, I broke into a run and couldn't help but smile. I was in love, and I was free.

With no classes to attend, the semester passed slowly. During the first couple of weeks, the RAs performed an abnormal amount of room inspections on Hunter's single. I'd jump into the closet, since they weren't allowed to open doors or your drawers. Unfortunately, Hunter had left two bottles of Vicodin on his desk. Prescription pills were being confiscated all over campus, but no one knew where they were coming from.

Hunter produced a doctor's note for the medication and got the bottles back several days later. He decided to lie low for a few weeks, and as a result, money was tight.

"I don't understand why I can't come with you tomorrow," I complained.

"Because my mom isn't happy about us right now. I'm going to talk to her and sort it all out. Christmas— we'll be together."

"I can't stand this. I can't go outside. I can't talk too loud. I can't do anything."

"Do you think this is easy for me?" he yelled. "I'm the one taking all the risk. What do you think is going to happen if they fucking find you here, huh? It's over for you but it's not over for me—I've got to go to class and get a job and get the apartment. You don't do shit here except whine and complain!"

"Then why did you tell me to come here?!"

"Because I love you!"

"No, you just wanted me here so you could be sure I wasn't fucking around."

This wasn't the second time he hit me—nor the third. It was, though, the first time I hit him back. After his hand hit my cheek, my right hand boomeranged back. My palm was red and couldn't keep still. I went to apologize, immediately sorry for what I'd done, but he was in no place to forgive.

He didn't apologize like he normally did. He simply told me to never hit him again, and closed the door to his room without kissing me goodbye.

The next morning, wandering through the kitchen, my whole world seemed different. This wasn't the kitchen where we ate macaroni and cheese out of the pot while we built our dream house. The freezer wasn't where he stocked my strawberry FrozFruit bars—it was where I looked for frozen vegetables to prevent bruising.

I took his hoodie and decided to go for a walk. November air has a way of clearing the mind, and with campus empty, I didn't need to worry about being seen.

"Rowan? Hey, Rowan!"

"Erin?"

Her hair was tied back in the same ponytail I'd left her with all those months ago. The harder I looked, the more I was convinced she was wearing the same basketball shorts, the same Voorhees hoodie, the same flip-flops-and-socks combo. I wondered if she'd known how much I needed her.

"Are you okay? Your mom called me last week looking for you. I didn't know you were back. Where are you living?"

"My mom is a stupid, controlling bitch, all right? She shouldn't be calling you."

"She sounded like she was worried about you. What's going on?" Erin asked, putting her arm on my shoulder. I winced and lost my hood when I shooed her hand away.

"Jesus," she sighed, covering her mouth, "what the hell did he do to you?"

"Look, I have to go. Just don't tell anyone you saw me here, all right? No one can know I'm here."

"Rowan, come back to my room with me. We can hang out and . . ."

I thought about taking her hand. If I did, one thing was certain—Hunter would track me down. I knew my punishment would be severe, but there was no telling what he'd do to Erin. Maybe the both of us could take him. But what would happen if we couldn't? I couldn't risk her getting hurt.

"I fucking can't, okay? I love Hunter and I'm never going back to my parents. Just fuck off."

I doubled back to the dorm and locked the door behind me. I drew the curtains closed, turned off the lights, and pulled the covers over my head. I didn't want to see anybody, and I didn't want anybody to see me.

CHAPTER NINE

"EXCUSE ME, can I help you?"

"I'm looking for the SANE Center."

I can barely hear the woman in scrubs who has appeared next to me, but her eyes are kind and she is smiling. I trust her. She tells me I'm in the right place and asks how she can help. Her tone is soft and sincere, and is enough to make my eyes fill with tears.

"Oh sweetie," she says, patting me on the back, walking me to the desk. "It's okay, you're in a safe place."

"There's something wrong with me," I sob. "I'm all fucked up."

"It's okay," she says, producing a box of tissues, and begins to look past me. "Is there anyone here with you? Is there someone I can call?"

"No," I say. "I'm alone."

As I watched Mom's blue Corolla pull into the parking lot of the Radnor train station, it occurred to me I hadn't been afraid till now. It wasn't because he stayed with me or because she agreed to come—it was because now I had to face it all. I'd made it this far, but I wasn't sure if I could go farther.

"That your ride?" Mikis asked. In the long wait, he'd given me his shirt, his name, and his purpose for standing in a train station in the middle of the night—his baby mama was in labor.

"Yeah. Good luck at the hospital. Look, I'm really sorry . . ."

"Nah, nah—I ain't gonna hear that. I'm about to be a father to a beautiful baby girl. I should be thankin' you for makin' me the type of man she can be proud of."

Mom was breathless when she emerged from the car—as if she'd run the 128 miles from the house on Elderberry to the station—and stopped when she saw me. Maybe she was afraid I'd changed my mind, or maybe I looked as bad as the night had been.

"Look," Mikis said, opening his arms to offer me a hug, "you take care of yourself. You call me when you get somewhere safe, a'ight?"

I nodded and hugged him back.

"Whatever is between you and your moms, just leave it here and start over. You don't need to carry that shit with you. Leave it."

I nodded, and turned toward Mom.

After running into Erin during Thanksgiving, the holidays came and went fast. We spent Christmas with Hunter's father Emmett and Hunter's grandmother. They managed a small ranch in Elizabethtown, near Clark Lake, just a half hour outside Lancaster, Pennsylvania. During the evening, we played cards and snacked on cheeses and deli meats. The room smelled of cigarettes, beer, and firewood, and Hunter never stopped laughing.

I remember running my fingers through his hair and

kissing him on the cheek before going to the bathroom during one poker game.

Emmett smiled at us and said, "That's a good girl for you there, Hunter. Don't be a fool and let her get away."

Hunter's mother Jackie was three vodka tonics deep when I first met her and she asked if I was on birth control.

"If you get knocked up, he ain't gonna marry you, I can tell you that," she warned as she went in and out of consciousness at the kitchen table.

She'd been through two husbands by the time Hunter was nine, and decided it would be easier to find a third if Hunter weren't around. When he turned thirteen, she shipped him off to Fishburne Military School. By the time he graduated, she'd married Lenny, a railroad technician with an irregular work schedule, who'd sign anything without reading.

When Hunter called to tell Jackie we were planning to stay at Emmett's for the summer, she began to cry.

"Well, I know you don't like Rowan, so . . ."

"What? Baby, I love Rowan. Any girl that makes you happy makes me happy. I just don't want her taking advantage of you."

"Mom . . ."

"Baby, I work too hard to be supporting the both of you. That girl has gotta carry her weight."

Jackie hadn't worked in over a decade. When Hunter was fifteen, they'd gotten into a car accident, and she'd been collecting disability, and Vicodin, ever since.

Eventually, she wore him down, and Hunter and I headed to Jackie's for the summer.

One thing I could never accuse Jackie of was not loving

her son. Hunter was truly the best thing she'd ever done with her life and she wanted me to know it. The morning after we arrived, she cooked an enormous breakfast. Hunter inhaled two huge pancakes, and knocked back a glass of orange juice, before leaving me alone with his mother while he went off to work with Emmett.

Jackie and I sat in silence for what seemed like a long time before she asked me, "Do you love him?"

"More than anything," I said.

"Bullshit. You can't shit a shitter, and girl, you're trying to shit me."

"No," I stammered nervously, "I do. I love him."

"He's got a future, you know. A bright one."

"I'm not trying to get in the way of that."

She stared at me hard, trying to discern if I could be trusted, before smiling and squeezing my hand. "Good. You know how to make a Bloody Mary?"

As the summer progressed, Jackie became my friend. We'd take her Mercedes to the salon to get her roots treated, her acrylics filled in, her Botox injected. We tanned by the pool and selected outfits we thought might look good on Hunter.

As the Fourth of July party approached, Jackie enlisted my help.

"The sauce is key," she said as she rolled the meatballs.

"Okay, where do I find it?"

Jackie threw her head back and cackled. "Oh, you won't find jarred sauce in this house, Rowan. Your mom doesn't make her own sauce?"

I hadn't thought about Mom in a while. Hunter had me call Verizon to get her number blocked, and set it up so I couldn't receive calls from private or blocked numbers. It was the first time I realized I missed my mother.

"No," I said, trying not to cry, "she buys hers."

"Bleh," Jackie said, sticking her tongue out. "Please tell me she doesn't buy Ragu or Prego." She laughed.

"No," I half laughed. "She gets her sauce from this Italian place by our house, Ceriello's. They have all sorts of meat and cheeses and stuff there."

"Oh, well, you'll have to bring me some the next time you go home!"

"Definitely," I lied, wiping a few tears away.

"Aww, baby," she said, setting down the tomatoes and putting her arms around me. "What's wrong?"

"Nothing. I just haven't talked to my mom in a while, is all."

"Well, why don't you call her?" Jackie suggested, walking over to grab her cordless.

"No, no. I'm okay."

"You know, Rowan, Hunter told me about your mom."

"Yeah?"

"I get it. Mothers are not easy. But you know, whatever it is you two are fighting about, I'm sure she'd love to just talk to you and see how you're doing."

"I know," I said. "I'm just not ready yet."

"Okay, well, the phone is here whenever you are."

As I showered later that night, Hunter burst through the door, and pulled me out by my hair. I tripped over the tub and my knees crashed against the tile. The curtain hooks snapped against the rod, as I gripped the shower curtain trying to steady myself before I lost my grip and my head became surrounded by water.

My breasts were crushed against the cold porcelain,

Hunter's fingers squeezing my hair, pushing my head against the toilet trap, before pulling me back up. I gasped for air and rubbed my eyes, trying to come to.

"Do you hear me?" he screamed.

"I'm sorry, I'm sorry," I replied instinctively.

"If you miss your fucking mother so much, then fucking go. Go!"

"Hunter, I don't—"

SLAP.

"Don't you fucking lie to me!" he screamed, pushing my head into the toilet again.

My wet hands slipped against the toilet, trying to break free.

"I swear to god, Rowan," he said, pulling me up. "You say you love me. You say you want to be with me. You say you can't imagine life without me, and yet here you are, using my mom to help you get back. You fucking hate your mother!"

"I'm sorry, Hunter," I said, slowly getting up from the soaked floor, and turning the water off. "I'm so sorry." I embraced him.

Hunter pulled me in close, and began to cry. "I just love you so much. Your mother is a fucking crazy, controlling bitch. She doesn't understand what we have and she never will, you understand?"

"Yes, I understand."

Before we left Hunter's mom's house to return to Cabrini after summer break, Jackie gave him $500 for textbooks, and told me to make sure he got to all his classes on time. I hadn't realized break was over until Hunter started packing.

"Senior year," she sighed. "No more second chances

after this, mister, so get your butt to class. What about you, Rowan? You excited about graduation?"

"Me? I'm not graduating this year. I've got one more year left," I lied.

"Well, enjoy it," she said, opening her arms to me. "I'm so happy Hunter found you. He really loves you, you know."

"I love him too."

"I gave Hunter some money for textbooks and groceries, but I wanted you to have this too." She placed two hundred-dollar bills in my hand.

"Oh, Jackie, no—I can't take this."

"Sure you can!" she said, pulling me in tight. "I know you don't have the greatest relationship with your parents, so take it. Just a little something to start the semester off right."

"Thank you," I said, hugging her back.

We stood there in each other's arms for a moment, before Hunter's horn pierced through our embrace.

"Take care!" she called out as I got into the car.

Hunter barely waited for me to close the door before peeling out of the driveway, speeding down the block, and coming to a halt at the corner. He said nothing, and simply held his hand out between us.

I bent forward to grab my bag, using my hair to cover me as I slipped one of the hundreds under the seat and put the other in his hand.

"That's it?"

"Maybe she doesn't like me as much as you think she does."

"I don't know how we're going to make this last," he said, taking a left toward the highway.

"It would if you didn't spend it all on alcohol."

I wasn't surprised that he hit me, only surprised that he pulled over to do it. We spent the rest of the ride in silence, until he made the turn onto King of Prussia Road. As was our routine, I unclicked my seat belt and climbed into the backseat to hide from Public Safety.

It had been a year since I sneaked out of the house on Elderberry. Things were good for a while. It seemed natural—like it was always meant to be just the two of us. But Mom was relentless. She called, e-mailed, sent letters. Erin was the first to tell me that Mom found her number in an old phone of mine, and was calling people asking for information.

I headed her off, calling all my friends and advising them not to tell her where I was, to say they hadn't heard from me, to lie. I got frustrated when people asked me why I was doing this, what was happening, if everything was okay. Of course I was okay . . . I was with Hunter.

Mom called Public Safety every morning, and also at three p.m. during shift change. "Yes, Mrs. Kelly, we're aware your daughter is living on campus . . ."

Mom and Public Safety shared the same problem— they couldn't find me. Since I was no longer a student, I was living on Cabrini's campus illegally, thereby also implicating Hunter for allowing it to happen. Public Safety often performed routine checks and inspections on his dorm, but we were always one step ahead.

Hunter's network of clients was on the lookout for Public Safety. They helped me out windows, down halls, into their rooms for hiding—anything to score an extra dime bag. Hunter and I would laugh at how stupid Mom was, how stupid Public Safety was.

Now, I wonder if I'd have laughed if I had known her hair had begun to fall out. If I'd witnessed the rapid weight loss, her sleep deprivation. I wonder if I'd have thought it was funny to hear her cry at night, at church, on the way to the grocery store. I wonder if I'd have thought myself a badass if I'd watched her examine herself, her actions, her existence, wondering where she went wrong—desperately searching for the answer as to how I could have gone so far off the path she'd so carefully laid out for me. I wonder how I ever could have thought she didn't love me, didn't want me. I wonder what right I had to ever claim she wasn't my mother.

And yet she kept going, for she knew I was alive, and she knew I was in trouble.

"I think we need to wash this blanket," I said, sitting up once we turned into the parking lot.

"Hey," he snapped, reaching his hand backward to throw the blanket back over me, "did I say you could fucking come out yet? Jesus, Rowan."

I lay back down, and waited for Hunter's Explorer to come to a complete stop before running into his new building, and up to his new room.

Knowing better than to touch anything or to try and go outside in an attempt to unpack the car, I sat on his bed and waited.

"At least you got a single this year."

"Yeah, that freshman in housing hooked it up."

Hunter walked along the perimeter of the 164-square-foot room, deciding where to place things. "So, I'm going to bring the stuff up. Just start unpacking the clothes and we'll worry about the rest tomorrow."

He brought in box after box of shirts, pants, and unmentionables followed by the posters, bedding, and the samurai swords he was convinced were authentic.

"What do you think of this carpet?"

"I don't know," I said, looking down. "It's okay, I guess. I like the blue but I'd want something darker."

"Me too. You know, when we get our own place I'd really like to have hardwood instead of carpeting in every room."

"Really?" I looked over to see him wedged between the wall and the dresser, no doubt trying to find the Ethernet jack, and decided to take the risk and sit down beside him. "What else are we going to have in our place?" I asked.

"Well," he said, dropping the cord and putting his arm around me, "I want a really big kitchen with a special display for all the chopsticks you got me."

"Oh, that'll be nice." I closed my eyes tight, trying to imagine it.

"Yeah, and upstairs we'll have, like, eight rooms—one for my games, one for your writing—"

"I get my own room?"

"Of course," he laughed. "You can't write with me or the dogs bothering you all the time."

"We have dogs?"

"Three."

He kissed me on the forehead and squeezed me before turning back to the Ethernet cable. Up until now, I'd been wondering if I'd done the right thing by leaving home. The year had been bad, but Hunter said it wasn't always going to be this way—that things were going to get better. He said my parents wanted to control every aspect of my life—that they couldn't be a part of my life because they didn't understand our love. And I believed him.

Rain came a few hours later. Most of the car had been unpacked, and the rest of the House 6 residents had arrived on campus. There was a knock at the door, and Hunter shooed me into the closet.

"Nick!" Hunter said, breathing a sigh of relief.

"Hey man," Nick said, extending his hand, bringing Hunter in for a handshake. "Rowan! How's it going?"

"Good, good," I said, coming out of the closet.

"What's up?" Hunter smiled.

"Just wanted to let you know Wayne's throwing a party over in the apartments. We're getting ready to head over—you guys want to come?"

"Absolutely! I'll meet you downstairs in ten?"

"Cool," Nick said, closing the door behind him.

"Are you really going to the party?"

"Yes," Hunter said matter-of-factly.

"I thought . . ." I began.

"What? What's wrong?"

"Nothing, I just thought—"

"Rowan, I can't just stay in this room with you forever."

"I'm not asking you to. I just wish you'd spend some time with me since I know classes are going to be starting soon and—"

"Fucking Christ," he said, slamming his hand against the door. "I fucking feed you. I give you a place to live and still it's not good enough."

"I didn't say that."

"Oh no? Well, you could show a little appreciation by letting me spend some time with my friends."

"Fine," I said, spinning on my heel and walking toward the bed. "Go. I don't care."

I took two steps before Hunter yanked my hair and hurled me against the door, the impact sending my skull forward, causing me to bite my tongue.

"I don't need your fucking attitude."

"I wasn't giving you one."

Slap.

I held my palm against my face where he'd struck me, trying my best not to cry. "I'm sorry. Have a great time," I said, kissing him on the cheek. I slid past him and took a seat on the bed. "I'll be here when you get back."

He slammed the door behind him without another word. I went to the window, and watched him and Nick take off toward the Cabrini Apartment Complex. I looked past them to the other students—some smoking, some laughing, some still unpacking.

Erin and I would have been juniors this semester. We probably would have gotten the same god-awful internship, and made fun of the people for whom we fetched coffee. I wondered whom she was living with—if she'd be going to Wayne's party.

I wished desperately for Erin to walk by. I'd tap on the window, and run for the door. We'd meet in the middle of the stairs and throw our arms around each other. I'd wipe away the tears from my eyes, apologizing for being such a bitch, and she'd forgive me instantly—telling me to fetch my things, and that we'd find a way to get me home. But the truth was that even if Erin did walk by, and if she did look up after I tapped on that window, I didn't know her anymore. I didn't know *me*.

As I stood there, I thought of all the things I used to blame Hunter's violence on—our living situation, his finals, the weather. He always apologized, told me he loved me, promised it would never happen again. Bruises had somehow turned to broken bones, cracked ribs, dislocated shoulders.

I was wishing for Erin because I realized what all victims of domestic violence know—eventually, my abuser was going to kill me. But more than that, I realized I didn't want to die.

I reached under the bed and grabbed the blue Kipling bag I'd run away with and threw it onto the bed. When I was in high school, I begged my mother for a personalized sweatshirt so I could match the girls in my class. But I never got one. Then, two Christmases ago, she found herself in Lord & Taylor, and what should be on the rack but a hoodie with *Rowan Rock* across the front. There was no way I was leaving it behind.

I took the $500 Hunter's mother had given him for textbooks, and filled the envelope with folded paper towels. As I went for the door, I dropped my bag and sat down on the bed. If I left now, I risked being seen by any number of people—Public Safety, his friends, or worse, a semi-sober Hunter. No, if I wanted to get home I'd have to wait until he came back, and take off when he finally passed out.

The sky grew dark, the hour late, and still I found myself at the desk, awaiting Hunter's return. I'd just lost my umpteenth staring contest with the ceiling when I heard the doorknob jiggling.

"Fuck, Rowan!" he screamed, slamming his head against the door. "Let me in! Keys no go in hole . . . fuck!"

I opened the door. Hunter was wearing the smile I once loved so much, and wrapped his arms around me. He kissed me tenderly, taking my face and hair in his hands as he did so. The side he'd punched a few hours ago ached under the pressure of his hand. He pushed me into the room, and we collapsed onto the bed. Hunter's tongue slithered up my neck and into my ear while his hands clumsily attempted to rid me of my clothes.

"Hold on, babe," I said, sitting up, "give me a second. I need to go to the bathroom."

Hunter pushed me back onto the bed, and buried his face in my chest. "No, don't go. I need you here."

"Hunter, come on. Stop!"

"Bitch!" he screamed, slapping his palm against my face.

When I opened my eyes, I saw my blood splattered against the cinder-block wall, and I vowed it would be the last of myself I'd lose. He pushed me onto the floor and took what he felt I owed him. The harder I struggled, the more I called for help, the harder he buried his hate within me. His nails wedged themselves deep into my thighs—tearing open wounds that had long since healed. Blood ran down my legs; tears down my cheeks.

Once he finished and rolled onto his side, I crawled away and leaned against the dresser and waited for Hunter's night to finally catch up with him. I crawled over him to retrieve my bag and was seized immediately. "Rowan," he said, tightening his grip, "get in bed."

"No," I whispered.

"What?" Hunter ran his fingers through my hair and,

for a moment, I almost believed I was wrong to leave. His gentle caress had once been preceded by kisses and laughter. Now, it seemed to carry concern and worry. Maybe we'd talk about it, agree to work on things—become better people. Maybe he would cry, apologize, and say something like, "I've never felt this way about anyone before. I just don't know how to do this. These feelings are so new to me."

I knew better. No amount of apologies and sweet nothings could erase the horror I was destined to relive in my nightmares. But waking from those horrors was worth fighting for. I suddenly realized I was no longer Hunter's. I hadn't been for quite some time. He wasn't afraid that I would belong to someone else—he was afraid that I would belong to myself. And so, I let the idea of our love slip away and repeated, "No."

"That's what I thought." The gentle caress I had once loved made its way to the back of my neck. He hoisted me up and hurled me into the dresser.

Blood invaded my eye. As I tried to gain my balance, he pinned me to the desk. "Is this what you want? You really want to leave after all we've been through? Where are you going to go, Rowan? Let me help you understand something—you're nothing. You hear me? You're fucking NOTHING! You think someone is going to love you like I have? Like I always have? Fine," he said, "if you want to go, let's get you out of here."

He rose to his feet and snatched my hair, yanking me toward him. I tripped over my resistance, and he dragged me and my exposed breasts along the hallway and out the door. I turned onto my back, thinking it would spare me more agony. My spine beat against each step, the rug beneath me burning hotter and hotter. As we crossed the threshold, the rain hit us.

Hunter brought me to my feet as we struggled and staggered toward his Explorer.

"Hunter, stop! Can't you see you're hurting me?" I wondered how far we were about to go. Were we going to the hospital, or was he leaving what was left of me for a morning jogger to find? I looked to the sky and wondered how we got here. There must have been some mistake—it wasn't supposed to be like this.

"We're going to do this together, Rowan. All I ever did was take care of you, and you show me no respect. You can go find someone else to take care of you like you always wanted."

In a sick way I wanted to end things there—with my arms around him, kissing in the rain. I wanted to tell him that all I ever wanted was for him to love me. We could cue the music and roll credits . . . maybe as the cast reel is going, we could do a montage of us going to couples counseling, getting married, and then cut to me in the delivery room.

But instead I said nothing. I was tired of screaming. I was tired of fighting.

He opened the back door of his Explorer and threw me in, slamming the door behind him. We whipped backward, and made off into the night. I managed to clip the seat belt around me.

Hunter didn't signal as we turned onto King of Prussia Road, and I couldn't help but think of my mother. *You have to use your directional, Rowan. It's dangerous not to—you need to tell people where you're going.* Hunter was going too fast for me to think about opening the door and taking my chances jumping out. We hydroplaned—speeding around every twist and turn. I looked over at him—his wet hair clung to his face, his shirt completely soaked through, his eyes still red from alcohol and fury. I pulled desperately at my seat belt—it had locked. All that was left to do now was hope—hope that Hunter decided not to crash. Hope that he decided we wouldn't burn.

When the car finally came to a halt, we were six miles from school. Hunter took me in his arms. "It doesn't matter where you go, Rowan. You belong to me. I fucking own you. I left my mark, and every man will know you're mine. No one will ever love you because I . . . I am the only one who loves you. So fucking go. Get off my campus and leave. Because soon you'll realize the world doesn't want you. I'm the only one that wants you." He placed the sweetest of kisses on my forehead before forcing me onto the cement.

My skin parted against the hot pavement as my blood cooled, soothing me, my body trying to reassure me I was alive. And then he was gone.

I lay there for a while—crying, screaming, bleeding. Part of me hoped he would return—that he'd still want me to be his. I waited until my eyes ran out of tears before rising to my feet, using the rain to wash the night off.

I inched, step by step, wincing as pebbles tried to become part of my feet, searching for what I knew was most certainly there. The paint of a set of double yellow lines gave my bare feet much needed relief. My blood grew a little paler as the rain fell harder. When I stepped forward, any evidence of me washed away. All that remained were my bare feet, the rain, and those two yellow lines.

* * *

Mom and I came face to face as Mikis's train pulled into the station.

"Is that him?" she asked, looking at Mikis boarding the train to Philly.

"No."

I don't know if she believed me. I don't know why she didn't hug me. I don't know if it was better or worse that we made the drive back to the house on Elderberry in silence. All I knew was I finally felt safe.

Dad was out the back door and halfway down the driveway before we pulled onto the blacktop. He damn near tackled me, wrapping his arms around my ribs, pressing his fingers in tighter and tighter, trying to make sure they hadn't come loose.

"I love you," he cried. "I love you, Rowan. Oh god, are you okay, baby? What did he do?" He wept, stepping backward, taking my face in his hands. "What did he do to my little girl? Oh god!"

Mom walked past us and into the house. After going to the bathroom, she put the kettle on, and took a seat at the kitchen table.

The first words I said to her were, "Where's Aidan?"

The first words she said to me were, "He's upstate camping with Jerry."

"You hungry, Rowan?" Dad asked, opening all the cabinets in the kitchen. "What do you want? I'll make anything you want."

"I'm not really hungry," I said, walking behind Mom's chair at the head of the table, toward the stairs. "I just want to go to sleep."

Halfway up the stairs, Mom called to me, "Rowan, about your room."

I let her pass me on the stairs, and followed her up, then down the hallway. She opened the door to my room. The bed was missing, and had been replaced with an Ab Lounge, two blue exercise balls, and a dresser that used to be in Aidan's room.

"You guys got rid of my stuff?"

"No, no," Dad soothed. "We just relocated it upstairs."

"In the attic?"

"You always said you wanted to live up there," Mom said coolly.

She was right. As a teenager, I'd always wanted to live in the attic, away from everyone. But now, going into my last year as a teenager, all I wanted was to be close to someone, to know there were other people breathing in the house.

"Just temporary," Dad said.

"Okay."

"And tomorrow, Rowan," Mom said, "we need to have a talk."

"Okay."

"No, not okay. There's going to be changes, there's going to be rules—"

"Yeah, Mom, I get it."

"Good night!" she snapped, slamming the door.

The days after were filled with questions. What's his full name? What are his parents' names? Where does he live? Did I go to the police? Where can we find him? But I gave no answers.

If I betrayed Hunter to my parents, to the police, then we were over. There'd be no way we could fix this, no way we could get back together . . . no chance for a future. Hunter was the only man who had ever loved me, and I still wanted to protect him.

After a few weeks, Mom and Dad realized I wasn't going to cooperate, and threw their anger and frustration into assessing my damage. They took turns shuttling me from doctor appointments to therapist appointments.

It was discovered that a wrist fracture hadn't healed properly—most likely from when I'd used it to block Hunter from taking a cast-iron skillet to the right side of my head—and I was put in a cast for six weeks.

In the beginning, I refused therapy. Then, about a month into being back at the house on Elderberry, I woke to darkness. The attic was black, the rain pounding against the window, and my palms began to sweat. I thought it had all been a dream—Mikis, being home, therapy—and that I was back in that room, waiting for Hunter to rape and beat and leave me. I started to scream.

Mom was shaken when she turned the light on and leaped into bed with me. I tried to fight her off, but she just wrapped her arms around me and squeezed. She didn't say anything as I screamed and wept and drooled. And when I was finally quiet, Mom didn't leave. She lay there, her arms around me, until the sun came through the windows.

It was decided I needed a routine, a schedule, boundaries.

The rules were the same as before I'd left. Mom had to know where I was going and who I was with. I was to be home by eleven p.m. every night, without exception. I was to have no contact with Hunter, nor was I to mention his name while I lived there.

"I'm going to be twenty in, like, two weeks. Why do I need a curfew?"

"Rowan, these are the rules. You want to live here, you follow the rules. It's not that complicated," Mom spat back.

"Aidan is eighteen, and he doesn't have a curfew. He lives here too. How come he doesn't have to be home by eleven p.m.?"

"BECAUSE AIDAN DIDN'T RUN AWAY IN THE MIDDLE OF THE NIGHT WITHOUT SO MUCH AS A NOTE! BECAUSE AIDAN DIDN'T DISAPPEAR FOR OVER A YEAR. BECAUSE AIDAN—" Mom took a breath to calm herself, or maybe she realized she didn't owe me an explanation of why things were the way they were. Either way, she also informed me I was to get myself to Nassau Community College, in an attempt to salvage what remained of my college education. Once my enrollment was complete, I was to secure some form of employment and go about obtaining my learner's permit because "we all have jobs and responsibilities, Rowan. It's your job and responsibility to get yourself where you need to be. You've made a real mess of things, and it's time to clean it up."

Then I remembered why I left—I hated the rules, the chores, the way she loved Aidan more than me. But mostly, I hated Mom. I hated how she blamed me, how she looked at me.

I didn't know she felt like she had to be hard on me, to be strong for me—that she refused to let herself fall apart until she put me back together. I also didn't understand that she was hurt, and took my actions personally, as if, somehow, the only way she knew how to show me love was by refusing me her tenderness.

* * *

People tended to say the same things. They told me Hunter was a piece of shit, that he wasn't good enough for me. But if he *was* a piece of shit who wasn't good enough for me, why didn't he want to be with me? If I "deserved so much better than him," then why wasn't I with someone who reflected that? Why was I always left behind?

The more I thought about it, the more I realized this went back further than Hunter and Cole and the boy I had a crush on in sixth grade. It started with BioMom.

I decided it was time for answers and put in a request for the files pertaining to my adoption. Two weeks after faxing my request, a receptionist called to tell me my files were ready for pickup.

When I asked for the address, I was surprised to hear New Beginnings Family and Children's Services was a mere fourteen blocks from the house on Elderberry, just before the Mineola train station. Since I was still without a license, I decided to walk.

I crossed over Mineola Boulevard after noticing the address was an odd number. As I walked closer to the train station, I thought there must have been a mistake—the red awning read, *Marchello's Law.* It wasn't until I approached the door that I saw four businesses listed in white vinyl.

Inside was a small atrium, and two doors on the left—both belonging to the law office. I decided to climb the carpeted staircase and immediately knew I was in the right place.

The office was adorned with pictures of Asian infants being held by white couples. A poster to the right featured a darker-skinned toddler and read, *Considering adopting from Pakistan? Let us walk you through it!*

"Can I help you?" asked the receptionist, whom I didn't realize I was ignoring.

"Yeah, my name is Rowan—"

"Do you have an appointment?" she said, turning her attention to the computer.

"No, I'm just here to pick up some papers."

"Do you have a case number?"

"No, I'm not adopting. I've *been* adopted." I could tell I was fucking this up by the confused look on her face. "I was adopted from here like years ago and I filed a request for my records."

"Name?"

"Kelly, Rowan."

After she shuffled some papers and started looking through the drawers, I asked, "Is it that folder with the Post-it on it?"

She snatched the folder and removed the Post-it angrily before asking me to sign for it. Once outside, I made a right toward the Station Plaza Diner. I pushed through lawyers from the nearby courthouses looking to grab a quick bite, and groups of nurses from Winthrop Hospital picking up lunch orders, and took a seat at the counter.

After ordering a grilled cheese, I braced myself for what I might find and opened the envelope: *Agreement of Adoption, Statement of Adoption, Initial Social History*— shit choice of words.

I had always assumed I was abandoned, which was why there were no instructions for my care. It was easier to think of her as an honorable mother, painfully doing the right thing.

My eyes scanned the top of the social history and stopped. *Park, In Seon*. She'd given me a name.

In means compassionate—*seon*, good-natured. Perhaps she came to know these things about me, or it was who she hoped I'd become. She had never found out, so it didn't matter.

My hometown is called Kyongdangnam-do, but Google asks if I mean *Gyeongsangnam-do* when I search for it. I am of nowhere and nothing. I scrolled through the results, hoping to recognize something when I saw it . . . I didn't.

BioMom's identity, along with BioDad's, are listed under the next section, *Background Information*. A patch of Wite-Out beneath a *CONFIDENTIAL* stamp covers their names—squiggles made with a black ballpoint pen are mirrored on the back of the page.

My grilled cheese comes when I get to *History of Birth and Admission*. I see stats on her period of pregnancy, my weight and delivery type. Below are two long paragraphs detailing my admission, and I can't help but laugh.

According to the bio-mother, the history begins.

My biological father was the eldest of four, born in the town listed as my birthplace, and became a farmer after finishing middle school. He is healthy, with a medium build, and has an active disposition. Reading about him in the present tense is strange, but knowing he could be alive is stranger.

My biological mother is the youngest of four, and worked in a textile factory after middle school. She is healthy, with a medium build, and has a poised, quiet disposition. I've never been poised or quiet.

They met in 1978, dated, and moved in together. She

got pregnant while they were living together, but *the disaccord of their aims and goals led to their separation. After that, she gave birth to the child, In Seon, on 5 November at Kao Maternity Home in Kyongsangnam-do, but felt that it would be impossible for her to raise the child for herself. Thus, she referred the child for adoption to this agency Jinju branch, on 6 November.*

I was collateral damage—clothes that hadn't made the cut into the carry-on, pictures and ticket stubs thrown into a trash can and left to burn. There was nothing wrong with me—I just wasn't worth the trouble.

CHAPTER TEN

"WHAT'S YOUR NAME?"

"Rowan."

"Rowan? Rowan, my name is Maddy—I'm a nurse here. You're not alone," she says. "You're in a safe place and we're going to make sure you get the help you need. Okay, you believe me?"

I nod.

Her eyes tell me her word is her bond—that even if she has to stay an additional three hours after her shift ends to make sure I'm all right, she will. It makes me want to tell her the truth.

"Now," she takes a deep breath, "what happened?"

"His name . . . his name is Cole."

Maddy tells me to take a seat in the first chair in front of the main desk and brings some tissues. She tells me she is going to make some phone calls, that she's going to be "right over there," that it's going to be okay. I believe her.

After what seems like a very long time, a woman in black scrubs and a ponytail meets Maddy at the desk. They look at me. Maddy shakes her head, and both walk over to me.

"Rowan, this is Sylvia," Maddy says.

"Hi, Rowan," Sylvia says, extending her hand. I do not trust her.

"Hi."

"Rowan, Sylvia is going to take things from here. She's one of the best SANE nurses we have."

"You're not coming with me?"

"I'm sorry, no—I have to stay at the front desk," she says, looking at Sylvia. "But you're going to be fine." She pats me on the back and motions for me to follow Sylvia, who is several steps ahead.

"Thanks," I say as Maddy goes back to the front desk. I never see her again.

I read somewhere the reason so many hospitals choose to paint their walls yellow is because it makes people think of sunshine and happiness. The exam room Sylvia takes me into is light blue and makes me feel cold. She motions for me to sit on the opposite side of the desk, while she slides into the wheeled chair near the computer.

"So, Rowan, my name is Sylvia and I'm a SANE nurse. Do you know what a SANE nurse is?"

I shake my head no.

"SANE stands for Sexual Assault Nurse Examiner. I specialize in patients who have experienced sexual assault or abuse."

I nod.

"Why don't you tell me what brings you here today. Maddy tells me you mentioned a man named Cole. Did he hurt you?"

"No," I whisper.

"Rowan, this is a safe place, okay? No one can hurt you here. But if I don't know what happened, I can't help you."

I don't want to talk to Sylvia. I want to tell Maddy it isn't supposed to be this way. Maddy would agree that Cole had played me. Maddy would understand I just needed to find one person who wouldn't leave me. Maddy would hug me as I sobbed and wondered how it got to this point. Maddy would know I need medical assistance to find the source of my dysfunction. Maddy wouldn't think less of me for giving my body to random strangers to fill the emptiness that men I loved and mothers who abandoned left in their wake.

But Maddy isn't here now. Only Sylvia is.

This is my chance to come clean—to tell Sylvia I'm not a rape victim, but that I've spent the past few months in the bed of any man who'd have me so I wasn't alone. That I let them use my body for anything—for everything— and I was scared of what might be within me. That I needed an exam, a diagnosis . . . an explanation.

But if I told her that, a bill from North Shore–LIJ would find its way to the house on Elderberry. I might beat Mom to the mailbox that day, I might not. But if I didn't, Mom was sure to open the envelope and demand answers.

"It's all confidential?" I ask.

"Yes," Sylvia says, placing her hand on top of mine. "Your privacy and making sure you're okay are my top concerns."

"You won't send anything to my house? My mom—"

"Rowan." Sylvia squeezes my hand. "The only people who need to know what happened here today are you and me. So." She takes a deep breath. "What happened?"

"I just wanted the pain to stop," I cry. "I didn't know it would be this way. I didn't want him, but, but . . ."

* * *

By the time I turned twenty, I hadn't seen Hunter in three months. Another one of Mom's rules was I had to be at dinner every night, Monday through Friday. After I dried the dishes and swept the floor, I'd go for a walk. Once I got to the end of the block, I'd take out my phone and call Hunter.

At the start of the call, he would say all the right things—that he was sorry, that he loved me, that if I came back things would be different. But within minutes, he was screaming.

"Why don't you want to come down here? You fucking some other guy up there already? You are, aren't you?"

I'd swear I wasn't.

"Don't you love me anymore?"

"Of course I love you," I'd cry.

"If you loved me, you'd be here with me."

I'd consider his words carefully. My wrist had finally healed, I had some money in the bank, and I had my learner's permit. But there were other things I hadn't had with him—a job making lattes at Starbucks, friends I went to the movies with, a home to come back to.

Valentina was still in Mineola. After I had finally gotten up the courage to call her, we'd met for lunch, and after a few minutes of uncomfortable questions and awkward apologies, it was as if I'd never left.

One night I thought I could muster the strength to leave it all, but I had to know one thing. "Where did you go . . . after?" I asked Hunter over the phone.

"I went back to the dorm and waited for you," he said flatly.

"And when I didn't come back? Then what?"

"What do you mean 'then what?'"

"Well, weren't you worried about me?"

"Rowan—I didn't wake up till like three p.m. I missed my first class because of you!"

"You fell asleep? After all that?"

"What the fuck else was I supposed to do?"

"I—I don't know. I thought you would have cared or been looking for me or at least worried—"

"You know what? Fuck you. You're not worth my time. You're not worth anyone's time. Good luck getting anyone to love you like I did—you fucked up. You're fucked up."

Like BioMom, Hunter viewed me as excess baggage that could be left behind. Maybe he loved me, maybe he was the one. But he didn't come back for me, and that was everything I needed to know.

I spent the next year and a half steaming milk and pulling espresso shots at Starbucks in the mornings and driving to Nassau to take classes in the afternoons. I'd come home, have dinner with my parents and Aidan, and head up to the attic to watch TV, fall asleep, and do it all over again.

I earned my associate's degree two months after I turned twenty-two, and went from steaming milk and pulling espresso shots in the morning to steaming milk and pulling espresso shots in the morning *and* the afternoon.

For the first few weeks it wasn't so bad. And then Miriam happened.

Miriam was one of those women who carried a Louis Vuitton bag but complained about having to pay sixty cents extra for soy milk. She was old, she was cranky, and she was a pain in my ass.

"Decaf venti nonfat no foam soy latte," I'd call from the bar to a crowd of angry and impatient worker bees.

"Are you sure it's decaf?" Miriam would ask.

I'd made it. I knew it was decaf. "Yes, I'm sure," I'd say with a smile.

After taking a sip, she'd say the same thing, "No, no. I'm sorry, this isn't decaf."

I'd take back the cup, pour the contents down the sink, and remake her drink as she leaned over the counter and said, "I'm deathly allergic to caffeine—that's why I need the decaf."

I wanted to tell her she was full of shit because decaf contains caffeine, but instead, I said, "Decaf venti nonfat no foam soy latte," with a smile.

"You're welcome," I'd mutter once she was out of earshot.

"I hate people like that," sighed a man one morning from the other side of the counter.

I turned to agree with him and felt my heart skip a beat. "Cole?"

I was beaming as I placed a kiss on Cole's cheek. I hadn't seen him in six years. The time hadn't aged him, and I was grateful. Even though I'd grown a few inches, he still towered above me at 6'1" and had traded in his Donnie Darko hoodie for a blue button-down. As I walked to the table, I smiled to myself—his green hair was gone. I'd never noticed he was actually blond. He was a man now, and single, according to Facebook.

"What up, girl? You find the place all right?"

"Yeah, I think I'm parked right next to you."

"Cool," he said, taking a seat at the bar. "You know, I would have picked you up."

"I am a licensed driver now, my friend."

"What?" he laughed, looking at me in disbelief. "They let you on the road?"

"Yup. I now have a driver's license and am legally able to consume alcohol."

"Hey, Cole, how's it going?" asked the bartender.

"Good, Jimmy, and you?" Cole replied.

"Can't complain. What'll you have?"

"I'll take a Blue Point and," he began, turning his gaze back to me, "what about you?"

"I'll take the same," I said.

"Coming right up."

"Okay, so you can drive, but are you legally able to rent a car?"

"No. But I will be in four years."

"Good to know you still need me for something," he winked. "Damn. A lot's changed. How long has it been?"

"Probably five or six years," I said, as if I hadn't already done the math.

"Oh yeah," he smiled, "at Journey's."

"Actually, I think it was at the Sadie Hawkins—"

"That's right, that's right! The dance!"

"I remember Sister Margaret Anne yelling at you because you were wearing sneakers."

"I don't remember that, but I do remember the nun with the unibrow coming over with the ruler."

"That's her!" I laughed. "Man, that was a great night."

We drank until my cheeks were sore from laughing.

He picked up the tab, and kissed me clumsily outside the bar.

"Take me home," I said.

"Yeah," he said, "okay."

"It's not that I don't like you," Cole said, looking around the room the next morning. "I'm just not looking for anything serious right now."

"Me neither, dude," I replied, tossing a pair of boxers at him. "Have you seen my bra?"

"Right here," he said, putting it in my hand and kissing me. "Last night was great."

"Yeah." I kissed him back. "It was fun. That's what I'm looking for right now—fun."

This is how the rules came to be—no more sleepovers, no meeting the parents, no strings.

Cole worked as a travel agent at a small agency twenty minutes from his house. He spent three months working fifty hours a week, then took the fourth month off to explore a place he'd never been, before returning to Long Island, ready to begin work again.

Before reuniting with Cole, I was seeing Jesse—a twenty-eight-year-old man-child not ready to make a commitment. Before him, Louis and I had been steadily headed in the direction of Facebook officiality, when he suddenly changed his Facebook status to "in a relationship" and changed his profile picture to one of him kissing a blonde he once described as "like a sister."

I wasn't expecting anything after writing my number on Cole's Starbucks cup and telling him to call me, and I didn't expect anything now.

* * *

Cole and I spent the next year fucking, smoking weed, and eating Oreos. One rainy day, I put on my sore-throat voice when I called Dan to say he'd be one barista short. I hung up halfway through him wishing me well, and headed out.

With the wipers on full blast, things were still blurry. The twenty-minute drive took close to forty. He was halfway to me when I got out of the car.

"Don't!" I said, as the wind took his umbrella. "It's not worth it!"

"Thanks for playing hooky with me," he said. "You want some breakfast?"

"Sure, what do you have?"

We ate Cheerios. I told him it was weird that my dad insisted on calling Corn Pops "Sugar Pops." Cole said he was normally a Frosted Flakes man, but the store brand sucked.

He asked if I wanted to listen to a new song. We lay on his bed, a headphone each, listening to Mew inviting us to go skating on the thinnest ice we could find.

We woke up a few hours later, split a box of pizza bagels, and finished off a pint of Ben & Jerry's with a single spoon. While watching 24 Hour Party People, Cole confessed he'd started listening to a lot of Joy Division after Tom shot himself.

"Yeah, I remember." When Cole first told me about Tom, I hadn't known anyone who'd taken his own life. And while I still didn't know anyone who had committed suicide, I knew what it meant to lose a friend.

"It was a long time ago. I just hope wherever he is, he's happy, you know?"

"Of course," I said. This time, he didn't shoo my hand away. "Do you miss him a lot?"

"He was my best friend, you know? Sometimes, I want to tell him things, but he's . . ." His voice trailed off as he covertly tried to brush away a tear. "He's gone. Linda, his sister, and I are close. Nothing happened, though," he said defensively.

"That's nice that you're still in touch with her."

"She's, like, all I have left of him, you know? I just wish I could talk to him, is all."

"What things would you want to tell him?"

"Well, I'd want to tell him about this cool chick I've been hanging out with," he smiled.

"Oh yeah? What would you tell him about her?"

"Oh, wow . . . this is kind of awkward because I'm hanging out with you too," he laughed.

"Fuck you," I smirked, hitting him on the shoulder.

"I'm just messing with you," he said, kissing me.

"Yeah, you're real funny."

"But yeah, Scott is my oldest friend but he's always with Patty so, you know. And Chris, well . . . I can't really see myself telling Chris about you."

"Do you tell *any* of your friends about me?"

"Sure, I do. Scott and Patty wanted to hang out before I head to New Zealand."

"New Zealand?"

"Yeah, that's where I'm headed next."

"Man, that's exciting! For how long?" I asked anxiously.

"Six whole months," he grinned.

"Six months?"

"Yeah, I thought I told you about this. That's why I've been working so much overtime."

"Oh yeah," I lied, trying not to be mad, "I must have forgot."

"Don't worry," he said, "we can still hang out until I leave."

We'd been "hanging out" close to a year, and only now did I realize I was not a factor in his decision-making process. He wasn't concerned about what would happen to us when he left. There was no *us*—and I wanted there to be.

"You should grow a beard, carry a staff, and pretend to be Gandalf," I suggested to Cole, a week later.

"I don't think I'd look good with a beard."

"Try it."

I'd volunteered to help him pack for New Zealand. Yet there I sat, on the bed, not helping.

"I don't think all this is going to fit."

"That's what she said."

"Do me a favor. Come here and sit on this."

"I just did."

"Don't make me make you come over here," he sighed.

I trudged across the room and dropped onto his carry-on.

He smiled as it lowered.

"All I needed was that ass."

"What are you going to do when you need to come back?"

"I heard women in New Zealand also have asses. There's no proof, but I'm going to find out. That's actually the entire reason for this trip."

"Fuck you." *Damn it, he makes me laugh.*

"Oh, come on. I'm also going to see if they have boobs."

"Whatever, dude. They won't be as good as mine."

"I guess you're right."

"What if you do, though?"

"Do what?"

"Find a New Zealand girl with a better ass and boobs than mine?"

"I don't know," he shrugged.

I wanted to tell him I didn't want him looking for a New Zealand girl with a better ass and better boobs. I wanted to tell him I was going to miss him. I wanted to tell him not to forget to write, and I'd be here waiting for him.

"Okay."

"Thanks for helping me pack."

"No problem. I wrote this letter for you. Read it on the plane."

"Thanks, Rowan."

I want you to come back to me.

"Listen, I better get going. I'm meeting Scott, Patty, and Linda at the bar. It's a going-away thing. I'm going to be late."

"I'll see you when you get back."

After Cole left for New Zealand, I quit Starbucks and briefly worked for a telemarketing scam before landing a job at the New York College of Health Professions as a receptionist. I'd finished up at Nassau, and briefly thought about applying to four-year schools, but was lacking in will and motivation. Part of me liked being able to count on things—direct deposits hitting my account every two weeks; a bacon, egg, and cheese waiting for me at the counter when the guys at the bagel place saw my car pull in; dinner with my parents when I got home at five thirty p.m. But the bigger part of me wanted to stay still so Cole could find me. It was about five months into his trip when Cole decided to come home, and he wanted to see me.

"Go with the pink," Valentina said. As one of my best friends since high school, I trusted her opinion implicitly.

"I don't know. I don't want to look too slutty."

"Yeah, but you want to get laid."

"True," I laughed, snatching the hanger in her hand. "Oh my god!"

"What?"

"I can't believe this is happening already. It seems like he just left."

"You going to tell him you want to be more than just friends?"

"I haven't decided yet."

"I think you should."

"I don't know—he just got back a few days ago and then I'm going to drop this on him?"

Valentina rolled her eyes and laughed. "You were fuckin' him for a year, mama. Should be *no sorpresa!*"

"I'm just scared is all."

"¿Por qué?"

"I don't know."

After he paid for dinner, we parked in Parking Field 4 at Jones Beach and headed toward the water, the August air cooling as we got closer to the shore. I helped him turn the lifeguard stand right side up, and took his hand so he could pull me up.

"I missed you."

"I missed you too."

We passed a bottle of pinot grigio between us, listening to the surf. As the wine moved through me, the question rose within. His arm curled behind me, bringing us closer. I turned into him, resting my head on his chest, the bottle between my legs, and told him, "Take me home."

He smiled, jumped down, and held out his hand. I passed the bottle first, then my bag. My butt scooted along the wood, and I stopped.

"It's okay," he said, putting out both arms, "I got you."

Cole kissed me there on the beach just as a state trooper flashed his light in our eyes, and told us we weren't supposed to be down there.

Before walking to the car, I glanced at the sand, taking note of how small my footprints were compared to his. Had the trooper not been right behind, I'd have stopped to take a picture—proof we had been there, together.

My pink top hit the floor the minute we came through his bedroom door.

"Wait," I said, as he tossed my $54 bra across the room.

"What's wrong? Are you okay?"

"Yeah, I'm fine. It's just—I don't know what this is . . . with us."

He laughed and shook his head. "Jesus."

"Look, when we first started this, I wasn't looking for anything serious and that hasn't changed."

He kissed me. "Then what's the issue?"

"I need to know I'm the only one. I want to be the only one."

"Oh man," he sighed, reaching for his phone. "I guess I better start making some calls."

"Fuck you," I laughed.

"Rowan, I'm not seeing anyone else and I won't if you don't want me to. But I'm still not looking for a relationship. I'll do whatever you want to do, though."

I knew the answer to Valentina's question. I was afraid because I knew he didn't love me—but I wasn't ready to hear it, and so I kissed him back.

The next morning, I woke up cursing white wine and the sunlight. I checked my phone—seven thirty a.m., I was late.

"Do you have any baby wipes?" I asked, climbing over him.

"What? No."

"I smell and I'm late for work."

"So take a shower."

"Here?"

"No, outside."

"Is that okay?"

"Yeah," he laughed, rolling back over. "Towels are in the closet at the end of the hall."

"I smell like dude," I called as the water came on.

"And this is my fault?" His voice was closer.

I heard the swishing of his toothbrush back and forth, and peeked out the curtain. "Who doesn't have baby wipes?"

"Well, I don't have a baby."

"They're a standard household item, man. Everyone has baby wipes."

"Maybe I'll get some then."

"No need," I said, retreating to the water. "No sleepovers, remember?"

"We didn't sleep the whole time," he said, pulling the curtain back.

"Maybe that's why they call it a layover."

He stepped in, and I didn't make it to work.

Suddenly, it seemed Cole was my boyfriend. We were going to dinner, the movies—to Central Park for the outdoor screening of *The Wizard of Oz*. Last year, we'd existed only in his bedroom, but now we were outside for all to see.

I remember wishing I had brought a sweater, but decided not to because we were just going to CVS and would only be outside for two seconds. It was November—we were high, and hoping to buy the last of the Halloween candy. I huddled close to him, trying to get warm, as he rubbed my arms up and down.

"Cole," I heard a voice call out. "Yo!"

Cole's arms snapped back to his sides, and he stepped forward, leaving me behind. "What up, playa?" he said, embracing the other man.

"Who's this?" the stranger asked, gesturing to me.

Cole began to mumble incoherently. He looked at me as if the thought that he might one day need to identify me to another person had never occurred to him.

"I'm Rowan," I laughed nervously, extending my hand.

"Oh!" the stranger smiled, recognizing my name. "Good to finally meet you! I'm Scott."

"Scott? Oh my god, yes—nice to meet you too. I've heard so much about you!"

"I know, I know," he said, doing an imaginary hair flip, "the rumors don't do me justice."

"Definitely not," I agreed. "Maybe I've been hanging out with the wrong guy." I nudged Cole to come out of his silence.

"Ah, don't let Patty hear you say that," he laughed. "What are you guys doing here?"

"Actually, we just ran into each other," Cole said flatly.

Scott and I exchanged confused looks.

"Yeah, it's so weird," I said, not wanting to expose Cole's lie. "I was just on my way to a friend's house. We're, um, having a movie night."

"We were actually just catching up and we were going to get some coffee."

"Cool," Scott said, obviously unsure of what to do next. "Well, I gotta get home to the missus. It was really great to meet you," he said, shaking my hand again. "Maybe we'll see you around sometime?"

"Maybe," I said.

"Cole, call me later, bro."

"Will do," Cole said.

I slammed the car door shut, and threw the candy in the backseat of Cole's Saturn in a huff. "What the fuck was that?" I scoffed, as Cole started the car.

"What was what?"

"You know what."

"I just didn't want it getting back to Chris, is all."

"Why don't you just tell him we're together?" I snapped.

"Because."

"Because why?"

We'd just turned onto his block, and I opened my door without waiting for the car to stop. I slammed the door again as he put the car in park. "Huh? Why?"

"What do you want from me, Rowan?" Cole spat back, slamming his own door.

"I want to know what we are."

"What are you talking about?"

"Am I your girlfriend?"

"Jesus," he laughed, placing his hands on his hips, looking toward the sky. "I knew this was going to happen."

"What was going to happen?"

"This," he said, holding his hands out to me. "This bullshit."

"Oh, so I'm bullshit?"

"No, this, that you're pulling right now, is bullshit," he said, walking toward me. "I told you I wasn't looking for anything serious."

"Then what the fuck are we?!" I half screamed, half laughed.

Silence.

"We're not friends. Friends don't sleep with each other for two years and then tell each other it doesn't mean anything. Friends aren't embarrassed or ashamed of each other when they meet people in CVS."

More silence.

"Like, seriously. What the fuck am I to you? Am I your girlfriend? Am I—"

"Oh my god, Rowan! You. Are. Not. My. Girlfriend. How many times are we going to go through this?"

That's when I knew I needed to ask. If I didn't, I'd get stuck in this moment, waiting for him. "Do you love me?"

"Rowan," he said, shaking his head, "Let's just go inside and—"

"No!"

"Fine!" he said, walking toward the house.

"So that's it? You're just going to leave?"

"You know what, Rowan? I fucking told you how it was. I told you I wasn't looking for anything serious and you said you weren't either."

"Well, my feelings changed."

"Well, mine didn't, okay?" he screamed. "My feelings didn't change—they're never going to change. You're not my friend. You're not my girlfriend. You are the girl I fuck once a week. That's all you are to me. That's all it's ever going to be."

I was quiet for what seemed like a long time before saying, "I think . . . I think maybe we shouldn't see each other anymore."

"Fine," he laughed. "Whatever. I give up."

CHAPTER ELEVEN

SYLVIA PUSHES MORE TISSUES at me, and tells me I have options. "Rowan, you are completely and totally in control of what happens from here. If you choose to have evidence collected, that's all it is. It doesn't mean you're pressing charges or anything like that, although you can speak to the police if you want to. Like I said, it's totally up to you from here on out."

I nod.

"Do you wish to have evidence collected?"

I nod. "Yes."

Sylvia places a consent form in front of me and says things like "blood and urine specimens," "sexual assault," "will become part of your medical record." I sign the form without reading.

She pauses to check that I've signed in all the right places, and continues: "Evidence collection can be an extensive process, but I'm going to be here with you every step of the way. If there's anything you don't want to do, let me know and we'll skip it. You're the one in control here."

I had cried. I had screamed. I had thrown things in a fit of anger. I went on a full-blown social media eradication.

Unfriended from Facebook, unfollowed on Instagram. I pressed the delete button on my phone with such force, as if the intensity would delete Cole from existence. I showered, scrubbing my skin red—determined to get him off me. And when the water ran dry, I recognized I was the girl lots of guys had fucked once a week. I used to blame them—calling them assholes, dicks, man-children. But the one thing they had in common was me.

When I told my friends Mom was getting me a math tutor to ensure I graduated high school, they made jokes about how it should come naturally to me.

I remember throwing my graphing calculator across our dining room table during one of Jamie's and my study sessions.

"I'm never going to get this!"

"Sure you will," Jamie said, retrieving my calculator.

"No," I laughed, "I won't."

"Look, don't take it so personally. Math isn't for everyone. Some people just aren't built for it—it's no one's fault. Maybe God skipped you the day He was handing out the math gene." We laughed as she continued to explain sine, cosine, and tangent.

I went to sleep that night wondering what else God had skipped when creating me. Was this why BioMom gave me up for adoption? Was this why Mom and I fought constantly? Was there a way to fix it?

This is when The Voice was born. It came to me in my darkest moments, times when I was most afraid and alone. It whispered and hissed, *You are not enough*. And I believed it.

As time went on, I learned how to silence The Voice.

It was most quiet when I was with a man. A man who listened to my stories, who held and kissed and made love to me . . . a man who wanted me. But The Voice was never gone. It was always there, lurking behind my ear like a rogue strand of hair that didn't quite make it into my ponytail.

And as I lay my head on my pillow, determined to put Cole and his words behind me, The Voice returned. It was loud and sinister and relentless.

There's a reason Cole left, it taunted. *It's the reason they all leave.*

As I listened, I noticed something—The Voice wasn't an external whisper like it had been before. No, it was closer, deeper. I sat up, threw off the covers, and began searching—through my hamper, behind the closet, under the bed. The Voice felt closer than it ever had and yet I couldn't touch it.

It's okay, Rowan, it said. *It isn't your fault—it's just who you are.*

Immediately I realized it wasn't The Voice I was hearing—it was me. The Voice was the part of myself I refused to acknowledge—the part that knew who I was.

All these years I thought I was trying to silence The Voice, but really, I was trying to deny what I already knew to be true: BioMom had regifted me like a scented candle reeking of gingerbread and sugar cookies. There was something inherent in me which made it easy for people to walk away.

The summer after Dad's best friend Floyd died, my parents rented a house on Long Beach Island, along the Jersey Shore. While Aidan and I were allowed to spend the money we'd saved on whatever we wanted, Dad always encouraged us not to buy anything until the day before we left.

"You never know—you might see something you like better and wish you'd waited!" he'd caution.

The day before we went home, I was in a gift shop surrounded by picture frames covered in seashells and necklaces with anchor and starfish charms. Toward the back of the store, there was a section dedicated to quotes painted on driftwood: *Life's a Beach—Enjoy the Waves; A Little Sand between Your Toes Is Enough to Cure All Woes; All You Need Is Ocean Air and Salty Hair.*

I was about to head up front empty-handed when I saw a large piece of driftwood. In lofty scripted handwriting, it said, *A man becomes a father when he holds his child. A woman becomes a mother when her child is conceived.*

"See anything you like?" Mom asked with a smile.

I shook my head, and we left.

As we continued to walk past the storefronts on North Bay Avenue, I wondered if BioMom had ever been my mother. Did she cry when she saw me on the ultrasound screen? Did she smile and clutch her belly when I kicked for the first time? Did she ever hold me? Why was I here, on Long Beach Island, with parents who didn't look like me and a brother whose blood I didn't share?

The Voice answered, *She cared enough to eat right, went to routine checkups, ensured your survival, and still cast you out. When she looked upon your face and into your eyes, she knew you did not deserve her love. You weren't worth it then, and you aren't worth it now.*

* * *

There is a short stretch of Jericho Turnpike where you can find hourly accommodations. Morse-like fluorescents whisper, *Your secret is safe with us.* Between doing lunch and coffee runs, four-door sedans that have seen better days sit side by side in the mostly abandoned parking lots. But by night, minivans and midlife crises wedge themselves between the white lines, having gotten lost on their way to the grocery store. The Hostway is at the end of this strip.

On Groupon, the Hostway Motor Inn is marketed as *a quaint bed-and-breakfast located in the heart of Jericho, making it a hit for travelers and locals that need a quiet escape.* If there's an area of the Hostway where you can get fresh muffins and a Western omelet, I haven't seen it.

I imagined the Hostway looked the same as it did when it was erected in the early sixties, at the time of its parking lot's first and only paving job. In fact, I'm sure the billboard advertising their thirty-five-inch cable TVs and free HBO enticed many Manhattanites in desperate need of a place to crash before driving the remaining sixty-seven or so miles to the Hamptons in the a.m.—their children immediately sucked into the gravity of the machine-that-produces-sugary-drinks' glow.

I couldn't explain how I came to know the Casual Encounters section of the Craigslist personals. I couldn't explain why I found myself there not twenty-four hours after Cole left me. All I knew was The Voice tormented me, and I needed peace.

I remember Valentina telling me this was crazy—that they still hadn't caught the Gilgo Beach killer—and asking what she was supposed to tell my mom when they found my body chopped into little pieces, scattered along the beach.

"I have a plan," I told her. "I'm going to wait in the parking lot and when the guy comes, I'll text you his plate number."

"Oh my god, Rowan! Do you hear how crazy this sounds?"

"I already know a lot about him. His name is Dave, he's forty-seven. Hold on, I'm texting you the picture he sent me. Did you get it?"

"No, no. I didn't get it yet. Seriously, this is a bad idea."

"Val! I can't just sit here, okay? I can't just sit here and be sad about it."

"Then let's go out. You want to go to the diner?"

"No! If we go to the diner, we're just going to sit and talk about it, and I can't do it. I can't keep going over and over this. I just . . . I need to do this, okay?"

Long pause.

"Valentina?"

"Okay," she said. "When are you meeting him?"

"Ten thirty."

"If I don't hear from you by eleven forty-five a.m., I'm calling the cops."

After missing the turn for the motel at 10:17 a.m., I almost hit some asshole running for the bus. He gave me the finger when I honked my horn and he smiled as the cars piled up behind me. The bus drove away with his grin and I knew he hated me. He sat on the bench while I waited for the light and he shook his head as though he knew where I was headed and what I was going to do when I got there.

In the empty parking lot, I wondered how to greet someone who promised you a spanking. Do you shake hands with someone who's asked if you like it rough, or if you prefer to go slow? Is it acceptable to hug a stranger you're meeting for sex? The answer is always yes, but I didn't know that then.

I wished I'd had a better reason—I wished headphones and traffic and *Friends* reruns were enough to drown out The Voice, but they weren't.

Dave was the first man I met through Casual Encounters. Something about his precise directions to the motel and how he reminded me to pick up condoms led me to believe he had done this before.

I remember he felt the need to explain his situation—how he wasn't with his ex, how his daughter was his life, why he couldn't have me at the house. I undressed as he told me, hoping doing so would demonstrate how little I cared about how we came to be in this room.

He talked me through how he liked to be sucked, and encouraged me take it deeper. I assume he had the same patience when helping his daughter—fractions can be such a bitch.

Dave was a personal trainer. The sweat dripping from his bald head as he drove himself into me tasted of creatine and PowerBars. He lasted an hour past the time he'd paid for the room but didn't ask me for cash—only if we could do it again sometime.

"Sure," I said, halfway out the door.

On the way home, I replayed our fornication in my mind, trying to transport myself back to that room. It wasn't the echoes of our flesh smacking together that silenced The Voice—it was something else.

Dave's hands had interlocked with mine. With each thrust, he buried the backs of my hands deeper into the mattress. And in his eyes, I saw his need for me was real.

His fingernails left half-moons on my love handles and he texted me before I could wash him off. *I need to see you again,* he wrote.

All at once, I could hear—the music from the radio, cars whooshing past, the cool air dancing with my hair. The Voice was gone, and *I* had returned.

Over the next few days, I surrendered to the giddiness that only comes from discovering that the boy whose name you've been scribbling over every inch of your notebook wants to take you to the dance. Except this wasn't high school.

I wasn't a girl and he wasn't a boy. He wasn't my crush and I wasn't his. He was a stranger to whom I'd e-mailed a photo of my naked body. A stranger to whom I'd offered that naked body in exchange for an hour's reprieve from The Voice's menacing persecution. A stranger who'd priced the value of that naked body at $43.71, plus the cost of gas. A stranger to whom I'd admitted his price was right.

The Voice was quiet in the days that followed. Dave texted me furiously, anxious to meet and mistaking my inability to sext for coyness. For a moment, I let myself think we could be something. I imagined where he'd take me on our first date, what secrets he'd tell me as we lay in bed together, how we'd lie to friends and family about how we met.

It took three days, but we agreed to meet at the Coliseum Motor Inn off Hempstead Turnpike, on the bad side of Eisenhower Park. Dave was doing abs and arms with some East Meadow housewife, and said he'd be there by eleven a.m.

At 12:15 p.m. I shot him a text: *Where the hell are you?*

Sorry, he replied. *Client is running late. Can we reschedule?*

You don't really believe that, do you? I thought to myself.

Fine.

C'mon baby, don't be like that. I promise I'll fuck you so good tomorrow.

I pulled out of the motel parking lot and drove home, trying to swat The Voice away from my ear, as if it were that rogue section of hair that never made it into the ponytail.

Mom was folding towels when I flung open the back door of the house on Elderberry. She didn't ask where I'd been or whom I'd seen—only, "Do you need anything from Target? Dad and I are heading over there as soon as I'm done with these towels."

"No thanks. I thought you'd be at—" I was going to say I thought she'd be at Nana's, packing up the rest of the house, when I spotted Emma's perfect, smiling face on a 5x7 postcard with matte finish. "So," I said as Mom went to put the kettle on, "Emma's graduating today?"

Emma was three months old when she first came to the house on Elderberry. Her mother, Mrs. Acosta, would drop her off at seven fifteen each morning before heading out to a corporate law office in Westchester, where she was trying to make partner. Emma's father, Mr. Acosta, came to retrieve her at six thirty p.m., after overseeing projects at his construction company.

Mrs. Acosta was promoted to partner shortly after Emma's fifth birthday. We only saw Mrs. Acosta on Fridays, when she came to pay Mom. Other than that, Mr. Acosta was responsible for Emma's dropoff and pickup.

When Emma turned seven, Mrs. Acosta began planning for college. Each afternoon of Emma's week was meticulously scheduled. On Mondays, Emma had tap and ballet. On Tuesdays, karate. Wednesdays were for piano, and Thursdays were for drama. On Fridays, Emma was tutored for the following year's math and language arts.

Mrs. Acosta coordinated with other moms to drop Emma off at the house on Elderberry after her extracurriculars. Emma would sprint up the driveway, eager to show Mom what she had learned.

Mondays were the hardest. She'd stand in the middle of the kitchen flapping and scuffing, kick-ball-changing and plié-ing, while Mom tried to get dinner on the table. Mom would just stand there, mesmerized by Emma's talent. If I tried to ask her a question, I was shushed.

"Rowan, Emma's trying to show me something—please!"

If I was trying to get into the kitchen, I'd intentionally bump Emma and laugh when she messed up her performance.

"You're just like your father," Mom would say, shaking her head.

"What do you mean?"

"You're a bully!" she'd laugh. "You're picking on a poor eight-year-old girl."

"I'm not picking on her—she's in my way."

"Please, Rowan," Mom would say, holding her hand up to stop my bullshit.

"Yeah, Rowan," Emma would whine, "*please*," exaggerating Mom's tone.

I didn't know I hated Emma until her high school graduation, five months after Nanny died.

When I came home from Pennsylvania at the age of twenty, things had changed. Mom had given up caring for other people's children, and was instead caring for her mother, whom we called Nanny.

Nanny had been showing signs of dementia, but they were dismissed as old-age forgetfulness. It was only when she started handing out twenty-dollar bills for Halloween that Mom and her siblings realized there might be a problem.

Following Pop-Pop's death, Mom's youngest brother, Danny, moved in to keep an eye on her. After two falls, one of them severe, Danny called a meeting and told his nine siblings their mother was in need of full-time care while he went to work.

Despite promising their father they would never put their mother into a home, eight of the siblings voted to banish Nanny to an elderly-care facility with a 2.8-star rating on Yelp. After a few hours of screaming, several door slams, and a drive around the block, Mom agreed to watch Nana on Mondays, Wednesdays, and Fridays, and Maggie would take Tuesdays and Thursdays.

Maggie lasted three weeks before calling Mom to tell her she "can't take seeing Mommy like this." Then it was just Mom and Danny.

Mom left the house at seven thirty a.m. and returned by six thirty most nights. She spent her days wiping Nanny's shit, feeding her baby food, and answering the same questions on a loop, which only ended when Danny came home. Some days were good, but most weren't.

Dad found it difficult to plan vacations. As executor of Nanny's will, Mom needed to be close in case anything happened. Cruises, or anything more than a few hours away, weren't an option. More than that, Mom found it impossible to look more than a day into the future.

It didn't matter what I asked her to do—go to the movies, grab lunch, get mani-pedis—I always got the same answer, "I'm sorry, Rowan—I can't plan anything."

In the beginning, I understood. But hate began to burn through me like a fever as I saw Emma's name scribbled across the calendar hanging in our kitchen:

Emma's recital—5:00 p.m.
Emma's play—7:30 p.m.
Emma's soccer game—11:30 a.m.

Mom was *my* mother.

"You can't go to lunch with me on Saturday but you can go to Emma's fucking soccer game in two weeks?"

"First of all," Mom would start, pointing a finger at me, "watch your mouth. Second of all, she asked me to go so I'm going."

"So?" I'd scream. "I'm asking you the same thing right now! Why can't we just go to lunch?"

"You know why, Rowan!" she'd yell back. "I have to be there for my mother. If something happens to Nanny, I need to be there, okay?"

"So you can't spend time with me, but you have

time for Emma's stupid dance recital? She's not even your kid!"

"Oh Rowan," she'd laugh, "are you jealous?"

"Yes!" I admitted. "I'm your own daughter and you'd rather spend time with Emma."

Mom would continue to laugh and shake her head at me. "Rowan, you need to grow up. It's stupid to be jealous of a twelve-year-old girl."

Nanny died on a bitterly cold morning in January. I was driving to get gas when Mom called and told me the news. By then, Mom and Danny had been Nanny's sole caretakers for three years. Toward the end, Mom would come home, slam the door, and cry. She'd cry and scream and ask God why her brothers and sisters had left her and Danny to do it alone.

Before going to meet Mom at Nanny's house, where they were waiting for the mortician, I stopped at Starbucks to get her usual vanilla chai and a black coffee for Danny. When I got to the house, I had to park down the block, since most of the spaces had been taken by the cars belonging to the aunts and uncles who'd abandoned Mom and Danny.

I think Dad, Aidan, and I believed Mom would return to us after Nanny was in the ground—that we wouldn't be bound by the threat of needing to be on call. But she didn't.

Mom was a slave to Nanny's estate—putting the house on the market, coping with the mounting pressure from the siblings to get as much money as possible from potential buyers, and clearing out the house.

The house on Harvard Street was still on the market

when June rolled around. When she wasn't on the phone with the estate lawyer, Mom was at Nanny's—cleaning and packing and crying.

On Saturdays, after walking to seven o'clock Mass, Mom would then head to the house on Harvard. I'd offered to help multiple times, but Mom insisted it was something she needed to do herself. Except for this Saturday.

"Can you believe it?" Mom sighed. "I remember when Emma was just a peanut, and now she's about to graduate from high school. Where does the time go?"

"When did she ask you to go?"

"I don't know—maybe a few weeks ago?"

"Let me get this straight—Emma asked you to come to her graduation a few weeks ago, you said yes and put it on the calendar, and YET we can't go get our nails done this weekend?"

"Rowan, you're twenty-three years old. You need to grow up and stop being so jealous of a seventeen-year-old girl."

"Yeah? A seventeen-year-old girl my own mother would rather spend time with than me?"

"Rowan, that is not true."

"Yes it is!" I half laughed, half screamed, pointing at Emma's name. "She's on this calendar, isn't she? You're going to be there, aren't you?"

"What is the problem, Rowan?"

I paced back and forth in front of our kitchen table, glaring at Mom as she dunked her Lipton tea bag in and out of her mug.

"My problem? My problem is she's seventeen fucking

years old and she still comes here all the time! She doesn't need you anymore!"

"Why does it bother you so much?"

"Because I need you!"

"You?" Mom laughed. "You've made it clear you don't need *me* for *anything*, Rowan."

I wanted to tell her I was sorry. Sorry for running away, sorry for telling friends to keep my whereabouts from her, sorry for not wanting the love she had given so freely in those early days. I wanted to tell her where I'd been and what I'd done. I wanted to tell her I was scared. I wanted to tell her where it hurt because everything always seemed to feel better once she touched it. But I didn't.

Instead, I climbed two flights of stairs to the attic, opened my computer, and began searching through the Casual Encounters for reprieve.

In the armpit of Valley Stream—before Long Island becomes Queens—The Stoner shared an illegal basement apartment with three men I never saw. He was slim, unemployed, and had a set of angel wings tattooed across his back. I'd cling to them while we fucked, hoping to take them for my own.

On nights The Stoner was unavailable, I slept with a separated lawyer from Wantagh, although his wife still had makeup and jewelry and clothes at their ranch off NY 135. When leaving, I'd have to cover my nose as the stench of seaweed wafted up from South Oyster Bay at low tide.

There was a grad student from Hofstra who once sprung for a motel when Dave was busy with clients, but usually insisted we do it in his car between classes. The last time we fucked, he offered me $300 to write his constitutional law paper and laughed when I asked why he had money for his paper but not a motel. "Honestly," he said, "no pussy is worth $300."

The farthest east I ever drove was to Huntington Station. He was an army vet with yellow teeth and American flag tattoos. I let him fuck me in the ass, and didn't tell him to stop when he turned me over and finished inside me. Two days later, Dr. Sherwin wrote me a prescription for Terazol 3.

Mom didn't question the tube of vaginal cream in my bathroom when she was looking for nail polish remover. She didn't wonder about why I came home smelling of weed and Domino's on days I spent with The Stoner.

And it was for this reason I blamed her. I blamed her for not holding me down, shining a light in my eyes, and demanding to know the truth about where I was going and what I was doing.

I blamed them all.

I blamed Cole for leaving me. I blamed the men from Casual Encounters for answering my messages. I blamed Valentina for not shaking me and saying, "Rowan, you don't have to do this!"

But mostly I blamed Mom. In my youth, I thought Mom had a network of spies reporting my movements back to her. How else could she discover I'd deceived her? But by twenty-four, I knew what all daughters eventually come to know: mothers know everything.

I blamed her for being able to expose my teenage lies, for being able to sense when I'd sneaked out of the house, for knowing my soul and my heart. I blamed her for not seeing my pain, not understanding she was simply trying to survive her own.

CHAPTER TWELVE

SYLVIA SHUFFLES PAPERS TOGETHER and stacks them on the table before looking at me. "Rowan, are you sure you want to proceed with the evidence collection?"

"Yes," I say. I need to know what's living inside me.

"Okay," she says, squeezing my hand.

She opens the cabinet above the sink, and I see a wall of white boxes. On each of the boxes, in bold blue writing, are the words: *SEXUAL ASSAULT EVIDENCE COLLECTION KIT.*

First, I open my mouth, so the cotton swabs can go around the inside, over my gums, along my cheeks, under my tongue. Next, I stand on a paper towel the size of a bath mat, and undress. Sylvia is looking for debris, hair . . . answers.

Men who aren't getting laid love you in a different way than men who are. They have one goal—to make your pussy return their love—and they will do anything to achieve it. They send e-mails detailing how their love will be proven. They send texts and make calls to ensure you know your snatch is loved and missed. They think about it in meetings, at their dinner tables . . . walking their daughters down the aisle. They'll never leave you.

The man I met before I came to see Sylvia was old enough to be my father. The possibility of actually meeting my father on one of these encounters had plagued me many times, but that fear wasn't enough to stop me.

"Hey, what room are you in?" I asked, pulling into the Hostway's parking lot.

"I'm almost there."

"I'm already in the parking lot," I complained.

"Relax, baby—don't be nervous. I'm going to make you feel so good. I'll be there soon."

I considered my options: Dave had his daughter this weekend, the married guy from Merrick was in California, and I hadn't heard from The Stoner in two weeks.

This guy didn't sound sexy. In fact, he sounded like a fucking perv.

"Fine, just text me the room number when you're here," I said, hanging up before he could answer. I didn't get nervous anymore.

By the time I'd agreed to meet The Perv, I no longer needed the GPS to get to the Hostway. I knew to make a right before the blue awning with white type, and to park my car in the back. I knew to expect the receptionist to be a bitch.

"Honey, you either gotta pay for a room or get movin'. You can't be fishin' out here," she said, one leg in the office, one leg outside.

"Excuse me?" I replied.

"You can't be sellin' your cooch out here, so either pay for a room or get lost before I call the cops," she said, less friendly.

She looked too old to be using the word "cooch"—a Virginia Slim 100 permanently attached to the corner of her crooked mouth, her hair the kind of red women flock to when they're trying to maintain the illusion of younger years. If she'd been thin, it was grandkids, three robberies, and countless whores ago.

"I'm not selling my cooch," I snapped. "I'm waiting for someone."

"Well, you can wait in your car unless you pay for a room, then you can wait in here. Until then, get your ass out of my peripheral."

The Perv knocked on the window of my Camry twenty minutes later. He looked like the kind of guy who is into weird shit and sweats too much. I hated him.

"Well," he said, licking his teeth, "aren't you a slice?"

"Did you get the room?"

"Slow down, baby," he said, eyeing me up and down. "Daddy just got here."

"Look, do you want to do this or not? I don't have time for this shit if you don't."

"Oh, you're a naughty girl, aren't you? Yes, I'm going to give you a spanking you won't ever forget."

He licked his dirty teeth as he backed away, and almost tripped over the concrete bumper block before turning toward the reception booth. I was disgusted by the way his socks fully extended up his calves, leaving only a few inches between them and the ends of his coral khaki shorts. The back of his blue shirt read, *Martha's Vineyard, Massachusetts,* and was completely tucked in. I imagined he and his wife purchased matching T-shirts on their Hail Mary pass to stave off divorce.

I checked the rearview to see him walking back toward the car, and I got out.

"Can you believe this place doesn't take American Express?" he said, fiddling with the room key. "I tell you, I've traveled all over the country, and every hotel—"

"This isn't a hotel and I don't care where you've been. What room are we in?"

"All business, I like that." He brought me into him, and pushed his tongue through my lips. It explored my mouth anxiously before emerging to lick the surrounding area.

The room smelled of Febreze. I undressed and began helping him do the same. He spun me around, bent me over, and thrust into me. Married men prefer it this way. Perhaps it's because their wives only let them do missionary, or because it's easier to imagine someone else.

Suddenly, he stopped. He closed the bathroom door behind him and ran the water. When he came out, he assured me he'd be ready to go in a few minutes. He fell to his knees and put his face between my legs.

"Do you like the way Daddy eats pussy?"

I noticed the clear plastic cups next to the ice bucket had just begun sweating. The TV screen was black, but I could tell it was on. His wedding band sat beside the remote on the coffee table.

I now became very aware that I'd found the man between my legs on Craigslist's Casual Encounters. I became aware he paid for this dirty motel room at an hourly rate so he could fuck a woman who was not his wife. I became aware that I couldn't remember all the men I'd been with and where I'd been with them. I became aware that there'd always be a new man, and never the same one.

I snatched my dress from the floor and pulled it over my head after I'd closed the door behind me. I hit the gas too hard, and my tires screeched as I peeled out of the parking lot.

I couldn't tell if my skin itched or if my left hand was simply looking for something to do. I scratched and scratched until the skin of my arm began to flake, and I was convinced there was something wrong with me. It wasn't the Febreze or the sheets or the man—I was sick. Some terrible disease was making its way through my bloodstream—growing stronger, killing me faster. I needed help.

So I went to the emergency room of North Shore–LIJ Hospital . . . for a cure.

I watch as Sylvia puts my shirt, my pants, my underwear into plastic bags and seals them. She uses a UV light to search my body, and gets more cotton swabs to harvest the secretions. She scrapes under my fingernails, combs my pubic hair, doesn't fight me when I decline an anal examination.

I place my feet in stirrups, scoot down on the table, and wince as she inserts a speculum. Sylvia apologizes as she scrapes inside me with more cotton swabs.

"You did great, Rowan," she says, rubbing my arm. She thinks I'm brave, but I'm not.

The phone rings and Sylvia answers. "The patient has an abrasion on the left vaginal wall at the anterior portion with a small amount of serosanguineous drainage. No, I don't think that's necessary. Yes, will do." After she hangs up, she turns to me and says, "This is the hard part, Rowan. I'm going to take some blood and I'm going to need you to give me a urine sample."

"That doesn't sound too hard."

Sylvia laughs a real laugh. "No, no—it's not that hard. The hard part is the waiting. Results can take up to two weeks sometimes. But don't worry. We're going to do a full work-up on you and then we're going to go over some things. Okay? You with me?"

"Yes," I say. I am with her.

"Now, I do have to tell you that we are going to have to do a tox screen on your blood. I don't want you to be scared, though. We're just checking to see if your assailant administered any drugs so that we can give you proper treatment."

"Okay."

Sylvia labels the vials of my blood for the lab, and waits for me to pee in a plastic cup. I know we're not going to find what we're looking for. When I come out and hand her the cup, she asks me to sit on the exam table again and rolls a tray toward me.

"Azithromycin to prevent chlamydia, ceftriaxone to prevent gonorrhea, metronidazole to prevent trichomoniasis. Next, Choice to prevent pregnancy—another pill in twelve hours. Combivir for HIV exposure, along with Viread, also for HIV exposure. Zofran for nausea."

I'm not listening, and she knows it. I take pill after pill, but some are so large and I find myself spitting up water and choking on chalky capsules. Sylvia tells me to fill my mouth with water, swoosh it around so the pill gets lost in it, and swallow. It's not working, and we take a break.

Sylvia places the plastic bags containing my swabs and secretions and clothing into the box, and places red tape on the bottom and the top. It reads, *SECURITY SEAL—DO NOT TAMPER.*

She asks me one more time if I want to report and I say no.

"You can change your mind at any time."

I take the rest of the pills, and Sylvia explains my follow-up care. "You can call the Infectious Disease Clinic at this number and make an appointment for no more than two weeks out, okay? You're going to need to get tested for HIV again and follow up with your gynecologist and GP. If you don't have one, I'm going to write another number for another clinic. Remember, if you suffer any flulike symptoms you have to go to a doctor right away."

Sylvia squeezes my hand. "I know this is a lot, Rowan, but you've been so brave today. You're going to be all right. Remember, you can call here any day, any time. I'm also including this sheet of support groups that you can go to if you feel like you need to talk to someone. Now, this is important: you have a ten-day supply of the HIV postexposure medications. Make. Sure. You. Take. Them. And get the prescription for the thirty-day supply filled as soon as you can."

Eventually, Sylvia stops speaking doctor, and tells me I can finally take a shower. I take off the hospital gown, kick it aside, and wait for the warm water to come on.

I stand there thinking about BioMom, Mom, Hunter, Cole . . . The Perv. I think about the men I've given my body to whose names I didn't care to find out.

As the water goes from warm to scalding, I force myself to review the specifics. I see The Perv's yellow teeth, Cole smirking on his lawn. Hunter parking the car in the emergency room lot. I stand bitter with hate, choking back vomit, and ask aloud, "How did I get here?"

I turn the water off and attempt to wrap the towel around my body. When I can't make the corners meet around my chest, I chuck it across the room and turn my attention to the scrubs Sylvia gave me. She said I didn't need to relinquish the dress, but I didn't need a reminder of that day hanging in my closet.

The dress isn't anything special—a pink-and-white-striped jersey-knit swing dress from Old Navy. Mom said she liked it when I came out of the fitting room, and the dress magically became worth the $26.99.

It suddenly becomes clear—*I* did this. I let the love of BioMom, of Hunter, of Cole, of all of them decide my worth. My wounds are the reckoning of my choices, and my choices led me to this—sitting naked in a hospital bathroom.

I hate myself, but I don't want to. I put the scrubs on and promise to love myself, to know my worth, to never be here again.

Two weeks shy of my thirtieth birthday, my family and I travel the four hours to the Boston suburb of Newton to bury my thirty-four-year-old cousin Alanna, who died of cancer. Arrangements are made for our caravan of twenty-plus to stay at the Red Roof Inn off I-90. In the lobby, Aunt Audrey demands that we change hotels and tells my father she is disgusted with our accommodations. That it's the sort of place that asks for a photo ID when you pay in cash. That prostitutes have lain in our beds.

I've gotten rashes from dirty microfiber and rinsed strangers' fluids out of my mouth using lipstick-stained Styrofoam cups from motels just like this one. I remain silent.

She and our clan make jokes about hookers and the

truckers who bed them. I can't decide if it's better or worse that, in my case, money never changed hands, and I allow myself to laugh along with them—I'm not that girl anymore.

I lie in bed that night, unable to sleep. I sit up, and begin scrolling through the Casual Encounters: *Married for married*; *Dom seeking sub*; *Looking to eat pussy tonight*. It has been almost six years since I left the SANE Center—six years since I stopped giving my body away. And I wonder if perhaps I am still not healed or cured or fixed. I wonder if I left the SANE Center that night knowing I'd never be able to make sense of why the woman who brought me into this world cast me out so effortlessly, that the answer wouldn't be found in the beds of strangers, that I'd have to be okay with the fact that some men and women need to adopt children in order to have the family they have always dreamed of.

Exactly one year, three weeks, and five days later, it is November 9. It is a Thursday, my longest day. I wake up at six to be at work by eight. At noon, I leave work and commute the hour and fifteen minutes east to study creative writing from 2:20 to 5:10. After class, I drive through rush-hour traffic, and arrive at the house on Elderberry a little after seven, stomach rumbling, head pounding, eyes closing.

I can tell Mom has been waiting to see me all day, for she is already halfway down the stairs by the time I unlock the door. I am tired, and am in no mood.

When I turn on the kitchen light, she smiles and says, "Give me your hand."

She is holding a silver Sharpie and is excited.

"Mom," I moan, "can it wait? I need to go to the bathroom."

Mom begins drawing a smiley face on her palm and holds her hand up for a high five. "This will only take a second," she says, grabbing my hand and pressing our palms together.

She laughs as I look at the silver smiley face on my palm. "What is this?"

"It's World Adoption Day," she says.

"What?" I say with a chuckle.

"World Adoption Day. I saw it on *Kathie Lee & Hoda* this morning. You're supposed to draw a smile on your hand and put it on the Internet."

She takes my hand and brings me up to her bedroom and begins to fuss with the DVR. "Here it is, here it is!" she squeals, clicking the remote.

As per usual, Mom has misunderstood the requirements. Each individual person is supposed to draw a smiley face on his or her palm and take a picture to post on Instagram.

It is then I realize Mom has never viewed me as anything but an extension of her entire being. That despite not being bound by blood, a family history of heart disease, or brittle bones, all I am has been given to me by her.

"You know," she says, eyes glistening, "you can still post that even though you're not adopted."

"What are you talking about?" I laugh.

"You were made for me," she says. "I was always your mother, and you'll always be my daughter. Didn't you say you have to pee?"

Acknowledgments

First and foremost, a huge and unrelenting thank you to my publisher, my mentor, and most importantly my friend, Kaylie Jones. Kaylie, you not only believed in this project and this book from the beginning, but you also believed in me. I don't know where I would be without your generosity, support, and wisdom. Not only am I a better writer for knowing you, but I am also a better person. You are my rock, my hero, and my dearest friend. I love you.

To Laurie Loewenstein, whose keen eyes, generous feedback, and countless edits turned this manuscript into a book. Thank you for never failing to reply to an email, answer a question, and provide encouragement when I needed it most. I am so incredibly lucky to have you as an editor, but even luckier to have you as a friend.

To Beverly Donofrio and the first readers—Jennifer Albers, Natalia Duran, Alex Grabovskiy, and Melanie Pierce. Without your feedback, suggestions, and sharp eyes, this manuscript would certainly have died in workshop.

To Johnny Temple, thank you for taking a chance on me and for providing the world with an opportunity to read stories.

To my KJB fam—thank you for accepting my weird, and never judging me for it.

To Jennifer Jenkins, my partner in crime, whose quick replies to eleven p.m. freak-out texts always kept me grounded. Thank you for all you do, and for all you've done—I love you.

To the team at Akashic—Johnny, Ibrahim, Susannah, Alice, Johanna, Aaron, and the interns—you are living proof not all heroes wear capes. You make it look easy, but I promise your sweat doesn't go unnoticed.

To Erika Anderson, Kevin Clouther, and Kristina Lucenko, who also believed in me from the beginning. Thank you for making me understand it's never too late to realize a dream, and for believing in me. Without you, I'd have certainly been an accountant.

To my loving parents, whose love is the foundation of this story and all I do. Mom and Dad, everything I am is because of you, your love, and your support. In my entire life, I don't think I'll ever be able to show the full scope of my love and gratitude, but damn it, I'll try. I love you both, today and every day.

And lastly, to Bryan, the love of my life, who spent countless nights listening to me read aloud, curse my computer, and held me while I cried—I couldn't have made it without you.